A MOMENT IN TIME

A Collection of Short Stories

SUSAN STOKER

D1157836

Three short stories by Susan Stoker, including The Boardwalk, The Other Side of the Story, and The Gift.

The Boardwalk- Walking along the beach one day a man meets a woman sitting on a bench. They talk and he takes her to lunch. But as most things in life, there's always more to the story than what meets the eye. The ultimate love story.

The Other Side of the Story- Kassie begins messaging Hollywood through a dating site. However, she's hiding way more than Hollywood thinks. Find out the "other side of the story" and why she signed up for an online dating site in the first place.

The Gift- Annie meets a new friend in Frankie and wants to give him a present...but she's only seven, and doesn't have any money. She has to wrack her brain to come up with an appropriate present. What she doesn't realize is Frankie is doing the same thing.

To sign up for Susan's Newsletter go to:
http://www.stokeraces.com/contact-1.html

THE BOARDWALK

by Susan Stoker

AUTHOR NOTE

When I wrote this story, I was thinking it was the ultimate love story. If this were me, I'd take such comfort in knowing I was being protected and looked after when I wasn't able to do so on my own anymore.

With that said, this is a sad story...especially if you've read my SEAL of Protection series. I had people tell me they hated this story, and that they regretted reading it. That upset me, but I stand by my view that this is still a love story.

I wish we could all stay young forever, but we can't.

If I have to get old, I want someone just like the Hero in this story by my side every step of the way.

Now, get out the tissues and read...if you dare!

~Susan

THE BOARDWALK

THE MAN LOOKED down at the fancy watch on his wrist. There were a lot of features on it that he'd never used, but it didn't matter, because the one and only reason he'd bought the extravagant electronic had more than once justified the cost he'd had to pay for it.

The cool breeze blowing in from the ocean ruffled his short gray hair as he walked with purpose along the boardwalk. His eyes swept back and forth from the watch on his wrist, to the ocean waves lazily crashing along the beach, to the many people out and about enjoying their day.

The afternoon was perfect. Blue skies, the sun was out, but wasn't too hot, and everywhere he looked were people out and about enjoying the weather. It was a special day for him and he was pleased the weather was cooperating.

There were strategically placed benches along the boardwalk, most of which were filled with young mothers and children taking a break, or older men and women soaking in the sun.

Getting tired himself, the man was happy to see one such bench coming up along his route. There was an older woman sitting on one end of it, her face tipped up to the sun, a small smile on her face.

"Is this seat taken? May I sit?" the man asked, smiling down at the woman. Her hair was as gray as his and pulled back into a bun at the base of her neck. Wisps of hair had escaped the confines of her hairdo and were blowing against her cheek and face, but she didn't even seem to notice.

Her hands were wrinkled with age, and rested serenely in her lap. She wore a pair of gray slacks and a yellow blouse. Both were simple garments, meant more for comfort than fashion.

She looked up at him and smiled hugely. "Of course."

The man sat down and put one arm along the back of the bench. They sat quietly for a long moment before he said politely, "Beautiful day today."

"It is," the woman agreed. "It reminds me of one of the best days of my life."

"Oh?"

She nodded and kept her gaze on the beach in front of her as she spoke. "My wedding day. Well...not my original wedding day, that was *the* best day of my life, but this one was a close second."

The man waited for her to continue, but when it looked like she'd forgotten he was even there, he cleared his throat and prompted, "Was it a vow renewal ceremony?"

She started then giggled and turned her head to him. "Yes. It was our twenty-fifth anniversary and my husband had it all planned out. He didn't tell me about it, and miraculously managed to keep it secret." A loving smile crept across her face at the obviously good memory.

"All our friends were there, just as they'd been at our original wedding. Not only that, but many of their children and grandchildren were also there. My husband tricked me asked me to go for a walk on the beach with him. I had no idea all our friends were there. They were all waiting for us when we got to the beach. Shocked the hell out of me, I'll tell ya."

The man laughed at the use of the expletive. "I bet that was a surprise. I can picture the scene, you thought you were taking a romantic evening walk, and then all of a sudden you were getting re-married."

"Exactly!" she told him, looking back out to the

beach, lost in thought. "But it was lovely. And for a man, my husband did a wonderful job with the little details. Everyone had coordinated and were wearing white, he'd bought me a new dress the day before, pink. The hotel nearby had set up tables so after we said our vows everyone got to sit down to eat." She sighed. "The picture of me and my husband standing by the ocean with the sun setting behind us is one of my most treasured possessions."

"I bet you were beautiful."

The woman turned and glared at the stranger next to her. "Are you flirting with me?"

He held up both hands in capitulation. "No! I recognize a taken woman when I see one!"

She fingered the necklace around her neck. "I might not be wearing rings anymore, darn things kept falling off and I kept losing them, so my husband got me this necklace instead."

"May I?" the man asked, reaching out a hand and gesturing to the large pendant.

She nodded and held it out.

The man scooted closer to her on the bench and closed his fingers around the unusual stone around her neck. "I don't think I've ever seen anything more beautiful."

"I told my husband it was too much. Especially to wear day in and day out, but he said that only the

4

most unique and beautiful pendant could do my beauty justice."

"What is this stone?" the man asked.

"Ammolite," the woman told him immediately. "It's made of aragonite, a mineral that's naturally forming in stalactites like in Carlsbad Caverns."

She sounded like she was reciting by rote, but the man didn't interrupt her.

"It's made of fossilized shells. My husband said it's one of the few biogenic substances in the world... made by life processes...or something. Anyway, he said it was perfect for me because it came from the ocean...and since he loved the ocean, it would be like I was always wearing a part of him around my neck."

"He sounds like quite the man."

"Oh he was...is." She frowned then, as if thinking about her husband made her sad.

Not wanting her to dwell on painful thoughts, the man dropped the pink stone back into her hand and changed the subject. "I can understand why you like to sit here then, especially since it brings back such great memories for you. I've always loved the ocean. It's powerful and deadly, yet soothing at the same time."

"Yes. I've never been a good swimmer, but I too have always liked being by the water. My husband was a fish. He could swim better than just about anyone

I've ever met. He and his friends would spend hours in the water, horsing around and joking with each other."

The man smiled at the affection in the woman's voice. He leaned back against the wooden slats of the bench and grimaced. His arthritis was acting up today and his bones hurt. The warmth of the sun felt good against his aching joints and he wasn't ready to go inside yet. He was eighty-six years old and no longer a spring chicken, but he'd be damned if he spent the end of his life lying around in a bed waiting to die. Besides, he had an important job to fulfill and didn't have time to be infirm.

He was still lean and ate as well as he could, not wanting to fill his body with unneeded chemicals and additives. He'd worked out every day of his life until about ten years ago when he'd had his knee replaced. The recovery had been long and he'd thought for a while he'd never walk again, but as he did with all the other injuries he'd had throughout his lifetime, he'd fought through the pain and overcome his temporary disability.

His face was wrinkled, as was the rest of his body. No longer the svelte and muscular man he used to be, but most days he was too busy to notice or care. Married himself, he took care of his eighty-two year old wife from the time she woke up until the time she went to bed at night. He made sure she ate healthy meals. Made sure she wasn't harassed or treated unfairly during the day, it was amazing how horrible folks could be to "old people", and he kept her company as she watched television or played cards.

He'd taken vows to be by her side through sickness and health, thick and thin, no matter what. Their lives were slowly coming to an end, but he couldn't think of anything better than spending every last second of it with his beautiful wife.

The woman he married was his life and he completely understood this woman's devotion to her own husband. To further the conversation, the man said, "I used to be able to swim pretty good once upon a time."

Her eyes came to him and he held back the grin as she eyed him from his feet up to his head.

"You don't look much like a swimmer," was her somewhat snarky response.

The man burst out laughing. When he finally got himself under control he said, "Maybe not now, but in my day, I was a force to be reckoned with."

"Not me," the woman said, smiling to herself and looking back the beach. There were several families with children playing on the beach and in the surf. She kept her eyes on the children as she said, "I spent most of my life in the shadows."

"Did you like that?"

She shook her head, then shrugged. "Not really, but I was used to it."

"I can't imagine that."

"Well, once I met my husband he wouldn't let anyone overlook me."

"As well he shouldn't" the man said. "A good husband does what he can to make his wife happy. And you look like the kind of woman who wouldn't be happy in the background."

"Looks can be deceiving," she said easily.

"You have children?" the man asked, noting the contentment on her face as she watched the kids playing on the beach."

She shook her head. "Nope. Never wanted them. But that doesn't mean that there weren't children in our lives."

"I'm confused," the man told her shifting against the bench, his back continuing to ache.

"My husband and I might never have had kids, but most of our friends did. Almost every weekend was spent with kids sleeping over so their parents could have a break. I remember one weekend we actually had thirteen children in the house."

"Thirteen?" the man mock shivered. "All belonging to one couple?"

She chuckled. "No. Four."

"I think I want to hear this story," the man said, leaning forward to stretch out the kinks in his back, his elbows resting on his knees, his head turned to keep the woman's face in view.

"Me and my girlfriends were sitting around complaining about this and that and how we never got to see our husbands as much as we wanted. It had been a tough couple months at work and they were gone more than usual. I got to thinking about how much I loved my time alone with my husband when he got home from his long absences, and felt guilty that my friends had to share that time with their kids. So I offered to babysit all of their kids one weekend after our husbands had been gone for a long time."

"That was a generous thing to do," the man told her.

"It was," she said with no artifice. "But I conned my other childless friend and her husband into helping me. So there we were. Four adults, eight little girls ranging from age thirteen to two and five boys, from fifteen to four. It was insane, but fun."

"What'd you do? How'd you keep them all entertained?"

"Water."

"Water?"

"Yes, water. Squirt guns, a portable pool, water

balloons. It was mayhem, but so fun. And bonus, we didn't have to give them baths."

"I can imagine," the man told her, picturing shrieking children running around a back yard with the adults laughing and joining in the fun.

"So me and my husband might not have had kids, but every one of my friends' children are special to me and we love every single one."

The man shifted uncomfortably on the bench once more. He had to move. When his bones hurt like they were right now, it meant if he didn't get up and walk, he'd be hurting more later. And if the pain got too bad, he wouldn't be able to take care of his wife. "Want to take a walk?" he asked the woman.

When she looked uneasy, he quickly said, "Not far. And we won't go fast. But my arthritis is acting up and if I don't get up now, I'll be flat on my back tonight. I'd love to hear more of your stories."

At mention of her stories, she smiled and slowly pushed herself to her feet and held out her hand to him. "I'd love to walk. Thank you."

He took hold of her hand and let her help him up. Once upright, he dropped her hand and held out his elbow. "Ma'am?"

She wrapped her hand around his arm and let him take some of her weight as they began to shuffle down the boardwalk.

All around them men, women, and children walked, ran, and rode their fancy scooters past them. The man kept them to the right, out of the way of the fast-moving traffic. The last thing he wanted was to have the woman hurt because of his need to walk.

"Any other kid stories?" he asked as they continued.

"Of course. Those kids are a handful, but hilarious," the woman told him, smiling broadly. "There was the time when Taylor got her toes stuck in the bathtub faucet. Her dad freaked out. He wanted to call nine-one-one but luckily his wife called me instead. I raced over to their house and managed to slick her up with enough Vaseline that her toes popped right out."

"Surely he was used to his daughter doing weird stuff like that. I mean, kids get into trouble all the time..."

"She was his only child, and he was very protective. He was such a manly man, but anytime his wife or daughter got hurt, he turned into a helpless mess."

"What else?" the man asked, enjoying the happy tone of the woman's voice when she talked about her friends.

"Me and another friend offered to babysit for another friend who had six kids. They were out of control that night, I'm not sure why. But by the time we got everyone in bed and they actually stayed there, my friends came home. I went home and told my husband how glad I was that we never had children, and we had the most amazing sex."

The woman had a comforting cadence to her voice. It soothed the man's soul. He was a happily married man, but he could listen to this woman talk all day.

"What about you?" she asked suddenly. "Do you have any kids?"

At her question, the smile on the man's face disappeared. He looked defeated and sad all of a sudden, but he quickly recovered, turning to the woman next to him. He patted her hand which was lying on her arm as they walked, and told her, "No. No children. Like you, I never really wanted any and lived vicariously through my friends' kids. And now their grandchildren," he said almost as an after thought.

"Grandkids," the woman said, tilting her head and looking off into the distance as they continued onward.

"Yes. There are too many to count," the man told her. "At the last reunion, there had to have been at least twenty of them running around."

"There was a time when I babysat thirteen kids at once," the woman said.

The man looked at the woman with an unreadable look on his face, then said hesitantly, "You told me."

"I did?" she looked confused for a moment, then said, "Oh yeah, silly me. Sometimes I'm a bit forgetful."

The man patted her hand reassuringly. "Don't worry about it."

They came to a section of the boardwalk that forked. The path to the right went down to the beach. The path to the left went around a smaller building which held restrooms then wound around to a large building known to locals as "The Establishment." It had apartments inside, a cafeteria, a small bowling alley, and a movie theater exclusively for the residents of the building. It specialized in older, classic movies.

"Are you hungry?" he asked.

"What?"

"Food. You want to go to lunch with me? My treat." He smiled down at her.

She looked confused for a moment, as if she didn't know what she should say.

"I'm married, remember?" the man asked quietly, holding up his left hand and showing her the band on his finger. "I'm tired and figure you might be too. We can have lunch then go our separate ways."

She nodded then. "All right. But I can't stay too long. I...I need to be somewhere."

"Of course," he agreed immediately, turning them to the left. "The food here is excellent. I think you'll enjoy it."

She looked up at the large building as they approached and relaxed against him. "I'm sure I will," she said quietly.

The man led them up to the front doors and into the lobby. A few people greeted them respectfully, but he didn't stop. He walked them into the restaurant and the hostess at the front smiled as they approached.

"Good afternoon. Table for two?" she asked politely.

"Yes please," the man answered.

Without another word, the woman led them to a table which overlooked the boardwalk they'd just been walking on and the ocean on the other side. He thanked the hostess and she told them their waitress would be with them in a moment.

"It's beautiful," the old woman breathed as she caught her first glimpse of the view. "How'd you know I love to look at the ocean?"

With a small smile, the man said, "I had a hunch." He helped her sit and took his own chair on the other side of the small table.

As soon as they were seated, a waitress came over to their table. She put two glasses of water down in front of them and handed them a one-page laminated menu.

"Hello. My name is Jessie. I'll be your server today. The special today is baked chicken, green beans, and potatoes au gratin."

"And dessert?" the man asked.

The waitress chuckled as if she'd heard his question, asked just as eagerly, before. "German chocolate cake."

"One of my favorites," the man told her and winked at the young lady.

She chuckled. "I'll be back in just a moment to get your order. Take your time." She patted the man on the shoulder, then walked away.

"She was nice," the woman noted absently. With a far away look in her eyes, then said, "One of the kids I used to babysit was called Jessie."

"Really?" the man asked. "What a coincidence."

"Uh huh."

"Want to make it easy and get the special?" he asked.

"What? Oh. Sure. I like chicken."

"Good."

As soon as they put down the plain menus, Jessie was there.

"We'll both have the special, Jessie. Thank you," the man told her.

"Two specials, coming right up," she said efficiently, then left them alone once again.

"Tell me what your favorite memory of your husband is," the man asked, thinking of his own wife as he did.

"My favorite memory," she mused. "That's a hard one. I have so many. Let's see…I think it was dancing to our song on our wedding day."

The man smiled wide. "That's one of my favorite memories of my wife too."

She hummed a few bars of a song the man recognized.

"That's an unconventional wedding song," he noted.

She nodded. "It is. But it fit us so well. I had the hardest time choosing a song. It drove me crazy. But the first time I heard that song, I knew it was meant for us."

"It's lovely."

She nodded in agreement. "What's your favorite memory of your wife?" she asked.

"I can't pick one," the man said immediately. "From our second meeting, I knew she was mine."

"Your second meeting? Not your first?" she asked eyebrows raised.

"As she liked to rub it in, the first time we met, I didn't really notice her. But thank God I had a second chance."

The woman laughed. "She sounds like a forgiving sort."

"Oh she is," the man reassured her. "But she's not a pushover. Not at all. She's one of the strongest women I've ever met in my life, and I've met some strong women in my time. She's selfless and giving and kind. You asked what my favorite memory of her is, and I lied when I said I couldn't pick one. It's the look of her peaceful face, asleep in our bed, then the look of love that would shine in her eyes when she opened them and saw me lying next to her. That's my favorite memory."

The woman's brow furrowed and she moved her gaze to the ocean in the distance. The man looked out too and saw a group of men running down the beach in shorts and gray t-shirts.

The woman's eyes lit up. "Oh look. Here come the soldiers!"

They watched in silence as the squad of men suddenly stopped and began to do pushups in the sand. Then they moved to their backs and did a series of sit-ups. Then they all jumped up and began to run again. Both the man and woman turned their heads and watched their progress down the beach. A hundred yards later, they dropped to the sand again to start the pushup and sit-up process over again.

"They do that every day you know," the woman said knowingly. "Without fail. Every day."

"They must be disciplined," the man noted.

"Of course. They couldn't become the world's best soldiers if they weren't."

"What do you know about it?" the man asked genuinely curious as to her answer.

The woman turned to him, her eyes sparkling with mischief. "I'd tell you, but then I'd have to kill you."

He threw his head back and laughed just as Jessie came back to their table with two plates piled high with food. "Two specials. You're in luck, the cook just took the rolls out of the oven, so they're piping hot. Be careful though, don't burn yourselves."

"Thank you, Jessie," the man said. "Everything looks delicious."

"Oh my, this is a ton of food," the woman exclaimed, looking down at her plate in consternation.

"Don't worry, whatever you can't finish, I'm sure the handsome gentleman at your side will be happy to," the waitress said with a smile. Then she left after saying, "Let me know if I can get anything else for you. I'll bring dessert out when you're ready."

"She's very nice," the woman observed.

"She sure is," the man agreed. "Shall we?" he asked, pointing to the food in front of them with his chin.

They ate in silence for a while. The man looked over and saw that the woman was merely picking at her green beans. "You should eat those, you know. They're good for you."

She wrinkled her nose. "I don't really like them."

He shrugged. "At our age, we need all the vitamins we can get."

She smiled, "That's true."

"I'm sure your husband wants to have you around for a good long time yet."

"True," she nodded. "He would expect me to clean my plate." Then she picked up her fork and speared several of the green vegetables on it. She ate the mouthful, chewing carefully and almost daintily.

"Is your wife a good cook?" she asked when she'd finished chewing.

He shook his head fondly. "It wasn't ever one of her favorite things to do. She did it, of course, and I always ate whatever she made for us. But now we usually eat out. Why spend time doing something neither of us enjoys. Life is too short."

"I agree. You look like you can put a lot of food

down. My husband would eat us out of house and home if I didn't keep on top of our groceries."

The man smiled. "My wife always used to accuse me of that."

They grinned at each other, then continued to eat in a companionable silence.

Just when they were finishing up their lunch, Jessie reappeared with two slices of chocolate cake. A smaller one for the woman, and a larger piece for the man.

"How'd you know this one was of my favorites?" he asked, not taking his eyes off of the sweet dessert.

"Maybe it was the drool on your face when you asked what we were serving for dessert," Jessie teased.

The man mock-scowled at her while both the waitress and the woman across from him laughed.

"I'm teasing. But you look like a man who likes sweet things." Her eyes glanced over to the woman on the other side of the table, before meeting his again.

"My wife always says so," he responded calmly, not reacting to the waitress's blatant matchmaking attempts.

She took the hint, and told them to enjoy their dessert and left them alone once more.

The woman managed to eat half of her piece of

cake, and the man was quick to ask if he could finish it off for her. As if they'd done it many times before, the woman didn't say a word, but pushed her small plate across the table and allowed him to finish it for her.

Jessie brought out two cups of tea and set them on the table, saying, "There's nothing like a good cup of tea to finish off a meal."

The woman took a sip, then exclaimed softly, "Earl Gray. It's one of my favorites!"

"Imagine that," the man said, hiding his smile behind the cup as he took a sip of his own tea.

Several moments went by. Moments where the woman's eyes were once again drawn to the ocean as if compelled somehow.

"What do you see when you look at the water?" the man asked quietly, genuinely curious.

"It's not anything I see. It's a feeling."

"What do you feel?

"Safe."

"Why?" he asked.

"I don't know," she replied immediately. "It's not something I can explain. But when my husband used to be away from home, I'd go to the ocean and pray for his safe return. Knowing he was out in the world somewhere, maybe swimming in the very waves I was looking at, comforted me." She shrugged. "It's silly, but being by the ocean always makes me feel closer to him."

"It's not silly at all," the man told her, tears glistening in his eyes. "Did you ever tell your husband that?"

She shook her head. "No. He worried enough about me when he was away from home. The last thing I ever wanted to do was add to that worry. Better he think I was busy and not worrying about him while he was gone."

"I doubt he ever thought you were too busy to think about him."

"Perhaps not," she answered thoughtfully.

"Today is my fiftieth wedding anniversary," the man told her out of the blue.

Her eyes came to his. "Congratulations."

"Thank you. I've been blessed with fifty years with the love of my life."

"Do you have plans to celebrate?" she asked, taking another sip of her tea.

He shook his head. "Not really. We have friends visiting, but that's about it."

"Not even a cake?" she teased.

"Maybe a german chocolate cake," the man told her teasingly.

She chuckled. "Well, if it's as good as the one we had today, she's in for a treat." She frowned suddenly, then whispered, "I can't remember how long I've been married to my husband."

Taking a chance he'd spook the woman, but wanting to comfort her in her distress, the man put his hand over hers on the table. "It's not the years that count, but the time spent together."

She nodded. "You're right. Besides, I'm sure my husband is keeping track. He's smart like that."

"He has to be smart. He snagged you, right?" the man teased.

"Hell yeah," the old lady responded snarkily.

They both laughed.

Then she yawned.

"You look tired," the man observed. "You know, there's a great quiet room here. I'm sure they wouldn't mind if you took a nap before you continued on with your day."

"I don't know," she wavered.

"Come on, let me show you. Then you can make a decision," the man cajoled.

"Okay. But I'm not staying if I don't want to."

"Of course not. No one could make you do anything you didn't want to. I can tell that about you."

The man stood up, repressing a groan as his joints complained at the movement, but he held out his hand to the woman, not letting on that he was in pain. The woman took hold of his hand and allowed him to assist her to her feet.

"Would you like to take a cup of tea with you?" the man asked.

"I don't think so, but thank you for asking."

"You're welcome."

They headed out of the restaurant and the hostess wished them a good afternoon. The man led the woman through the old-fashioned lobby, down a long hallway with doors on either side, to a door at the end. The word "library" was on a plaque on the door. He opened it and they stepped into the room.

He led the woman past a table where an older couple was playing cards. Past a sitting area with a small television and four people sitting around on chairs and a couch watching. Past three tall shelves filled with books and a small table with a large comfortable looking office chair to an armchair in an alcove. It was sitting next to a large window, once again facing the ocean.

"Oh, how lovely," the woman exclaimed.

The man smiled. "I thought you might like this spot."

"I do, it's wonderful. And that chair looks divine. Well used and comfortable."

"Imagine that," the man murmured. Then louder he said, "Have a seat."

She nodded and he helped her ease herself into the comfortable leather chair. The cushion engulfed her slight frame and she settled back as if she'd done it a thousand times before.

The man leaned over and pushed a footstool closer to the chair, then lifted the woman's feet until they rested on the leather cushion.

She groaned in ecstasy as she leaned back into the chair and closed her eyes. "This feels wonderful," she said quietly.

"Go ahead a take a nap," the man told her.

Her eyes popped open. "Oh, but I need to get home and make sure dinner is on the table for my husband."

"I'm sure you'll be up in an hour or two. You'll have plenty of time to get home to your husband."

She nodded. "Yeah, you're right. I'll feel so much better when I wake up I'm sure."

"Sleep well," the man told her softly.

"Ummm," was the woman's response. She'd turned her head and was gazing out the window at the waves rolling onto the beach once more.

The man backed up, not taking his eyes from the woman in the chair. He went around the corner and sat down at the small table they'd passed earlier. The chair had a well-worn pad on it and even though there were many people milling about, none had claimed the obviously comfortable and peaceful spot where the man now sat.

Several minutes went by before the waitress from the restaurant appeared next to the table.

"Can I sit?"

The man nodded and gestured with his head to the chair next to him.

Jessie pulled it out, careful not to make any noise so she didn't wake the sleeping woman around the corner.

"She get settled?"

The man nodded.

"Grandpop and the others will be here in about an hour," Jessie informed the man. "You think she'll still be sleeping?"

Matthew "Wolf" Steel looked at the young woman sitting next to him. She was the spitting image of her grandmother. "She'll sleep throughout the afternoon," he told the woman. Jessie was his good friend, Kason "Benny" Sawyer's granddaughter. He and his wife had birthed six children before Jessyka had called it quits. All six children had been as fertile as their parents and Benny and Jessyka now had over fifteen grandchildren.

One of which was Jessie, who worked at the retirement home as a server in the cafeteria. The home was set up to look and feel more like a hotel, than an old-folks home. Research over the years had shown that elderly residents felt better about themselves and were healthier as a result if they lived in a less clinical and depressing setting.

They'd transformed the typical cafeteria into a restaurant. Complete with a hostess and waitresses. Residents got to choose what they wanted to eat from a daily menu and of course there were no bills delivered at the end of the meal.

"By the way," Jessie said softly, "Happy anniversary."

"Thanks, kid," Wolf told her.

"Does she know?"

"That it's our anniversary? No," Wolf said sadly.

"She's having a bad day," Jessie said. It wasn't a question.

"No worse than some she's had lately."

"The tracking device in her necklace is working as Grampa Tex meant for it to though, right? That's how you found her today?"

Wolf nodded. "I took a pain pill last night and by the time I got up this morning, she was already gone."

"Good thing you have that fancy watch, huh?" Jessie teased.

"It's ugly as sin, but it leads me right to her," Wolf agreed.

"You know you don't have to live here, Grampa Wolf," Jessie said, telling him something he knew.

Wolf replied with the same thing he said every time one of his friends, or their kids, or *their* kids tried to convince him to move out of the home. "She's my Caroline. I spent way too much of our marriage apart from her. I'm not gong to miss a minute now."

"But she doesn't know you," Jessie said, clearly not understanding.

"But I know her," Wolf returned. "I've always protected her. Always. And I'm not about to stop now."

Jessie leaned over and brushed her lips against his wrinkled cheek. "I hope I can someday find a man who is as devoted to me as you are to your wife."

"Me too, Jessie. Me too."

They smiled at each other for a moment before Wolf said, "Thanks for the cake."

"You're welcome. I'm just glad you could share your anniversary cake with your wife."

"She liked it didn't she?" Wolf asked, a tender look on his face as he recalled the look of enjoyment on his wife's face as she ate their anniversary cake.

"She did. But your friends are going to wonder why there are two pieces missing from the cake."

Wolf shook his head. "No they won't." And they

wouldn't either. Abe, Cookie, Mozart, Dude, Benny, and Tex would absolutely understand. They'd been as devastated as Wolf had been when Caroline had been diagnosed with Alzheimer's.

The disease had slowly taken over her mind, leaving her lost in the past and not knowing who her husband was, or even the women who'd been her friends for too many years to count. But they still came to visit. All the time. They'd pretend to be strangers and they'd sit with Caroline letting her reminisce about her "husband and friends," never letting on that she was talking with one of those good friends.

Before she'd completely lost her memory, Caroline had tried to get him to promise to move on with his life when she no longer remembered him, and he'd finally relented and told her he would. But he'd lied. He could no more move on with his life without her than he could breathe underwater.

Every now and then she'd say or do something that was so bittersweet it almost brought him to his knees...like today when she'd told him she used to stand by the sea and pray for his safe return from missions.

When she'd gotten ill, he'd researched long and hard, with Tex's help, and they'd decided on The Establishment. It had a great reputation, and more importantly, it was by the ocean since she loved it so much. He'd had her pendant fitted with a tracking device and had made himself her protector. All day, every day, he'd watch over his wife. Making sure she ate, slept, and didn't wander off and get lost. It was a condition of her being able to live at The Establishment. It wasn't a dementia or Alzheimer's specialized home. But they'd let him and Caroline in. In part because of his service to his country, the owner was also a Veteran, but mostly because he'd vowed to take responsibility of his wife's well-being and safety should she wander off.

Caroline's private room had one picture of him in it. It was from their twenty-fifth anniversary when they'd renewed their vows. Wolf was pleased as he could be that she'd remembered it so clearly today, of all days. It had been a wonderful anniversary present, even if she didn't know she'd given it to him. The picture on a shelf in her room was of the two of them standing by the ocean just as she'd described it to him earlier. She was in her pink dress, he was in jeans and a navy blue shirt. The sun was setting behind them and they were in each others' arms. She'd thrown her head back to laugh at something he'd said, he couldn't remember now what it was, and the photographer had caught the moment on film.

In the picture, Wolf was looking down at his wife,

smiling huge, the love easy to see in his dark eyes. It was his all time favorite picture of the two of them and he was glad she still had that memory, even if she didn't have any others from the last seven years or so.

They'd lived a long full life, and he was grateful.

"I'll make sure someone is watching over her so you can go and change. We'll meet you in the common room downstairs."

Wolf nodded at Jessie. He and Caroline might never've had children, but all of his teammates' kids had adopted them as unofficial parents. It felt nice. And today most of them were coming to celebrate his anniversary and to visit.

Abe and Alabama's kids, Brinique, Davisa, Tommy, and Kate. Mozart and Summer's children, April and Sam Junior. Benny and Jessyka's brood, John, Sara, Callie, James, Matthew, and Jessie. Dude and Cheyenne's daughter, Taylor. And of course Tex and Melody's daughters, Akilah and Hope.

Wolf was sure they'd all bring some of their own children too. It was going to be a huge, insane party which would probably disturb most of the other residents of the home. But Wolf didn't care. He and Caroline had made it fifty years together. Against all odds, they'd made it.

Wolf stood up and kissed the top of Jessie's head as he did. "Thanks for being so great with my wife."

"I love her," was Jessie's quick response. "You guys might not be my grandparents by blood, but I love you just the same."

The pesky tears sprang into Wolf's eyes again but he blinked them back. Dang he hated getting old, especially because it seemed like he couldn't hold his emotions back as he once could. Even though he was closing in on ninety, he would always be the alpha badass he once was.

"Whatever. Go. I want to say good-bye to my wife."

"Okay. Later," Jessie said, then kissed his cheek again, and headed out of the library to make sure all was ready for the huge party that was going to commence in an hour.

Wolf limped back around the corner to gaze down at his wife.

Caroline was sound asleep, her mouth slightly open, her breathing deep and even. He gazed up at the framed certificate and medal above her head on the wall. This alcove was Caroline's spot. The other residents knew it, and never sat there. Wolf had brought her favorite chair from their home as well as some other small touches from a life she no longer remembered. He wanted her to be as comfortable as possible in her new home.

He gazed at the Secretary of Defense Medal for

Valor she'd been given thirty years ago. It was the highest civilian award for valor and was created after the horrific September 11th attacks so long ago. It was Dude's daughter, Taylor, who'd asked one day if she could nominate Caroline for the honor based on her actions on the day she'd alerted Wolf and his teammates to the terrorist plot to drug the ice on the plane they'd been on. That had led to a whole lot of other horrible stuff happening to his wife, but ultimately, the terrorists had been thwarted.

Wolf had given his blessing, and with Taylor's determination, and the help of Wolf's former commander, Patrick Hurt, Caroline had been invited to come to Washington DC to be honored. The medal recognized private citizens who performed an act of heroism with voluntary risk to their personal safety in the face of danger.

Caroline had been embarrassed about all the hoopla, and had convinced Fiona, Cookie's wife, to travel to Washington with them so they could go shopping afterwards.

But Wolf would never forget that day and what she'd done. After all, it was the day he first laid eyes on the woman who he loved more than life itself. He'd had her medal and certificate framed and placed on the wall in her special alcove. Caroline had never asked about it, never even acted like she knew it was there, but Wolf knew. And the kids and grandkids of his teammates would ensure it always stayed on the wall and her actions that day would never be forgotten.

Caroline shifted in the chair and Wolf picked up her favorite fuzzy blanket draped over a rack nearby and covered up his wife's legs. He didn't want her to take a chill.

She was still so beautiful. Yes, they were old and wrinkled now, but Wolf could still see his wife's understated beauty shining out from her as if a light in the darkness. He leaned over and gently kissed her forehead, leaving his lips on her skin for a long moment.

He missed her. Missed his Ice. The only times he got to touch her was when he played a part, as he had today, of a concerned stranger. And even then they were only fleeting touches. But she was alive. And every day he got to take care of her. Protect her. Look at her. It was more than a lot of couples got and he wouldn't change one minute of their time together.

"I love you, Ice," he said softly. "Happy Anniversary. I'll find you tomorrow by the ocean and we'll reminisce about our twenty-fifth anniversary. We'll hum the melody to *Come with Me* together. We'll talk about your friends and the children who you loved as your own. Then we'll do it all again the next day. And the next. Until the day I die, I'll be here by your side."

Caroline's eyes opened without warning, and Wolf pulled back, not wanting to frighten her. And waking up with a stranger hovering over her *would* scare her.

"Matthew?" she asked softly.

And the pesky tears he'd managed to beat back sprung right back into his eyes at her whispered word. His wife hadn't said his name in over two years. *Two years.*

"Yeah, Ice, it's me."

"I love you."

"I love you, too."

A small sweet smile spread across her lips and her eyes closed.

"Sleep well, my love," Wolf told her, openly crying now, not even trying to check the tears which ran down his wrinkled face.

"I always sleep well knowing you're watching over me," she whispered. Then moments later her chest was moving up and down in the rhythmic motions of sleep.

The tears wouldn't stop. He'd just witnessed a miracle. The doctors had said she'd most likely never recognize him again. She was lost in her memories.

He sat up and wiped his face with his hands and

finally smiled. His wife had just given him the best present she'd ever gifted him with. On their anniversary no less.

Brushing his hand over her hair gently, tucking a stray lock behind her ear, he said softly, "I'll always watch over you, Caroline. Until tomorrow."

Then the old man kissed two fingers, gently touched them to the woman's mouth, and walked out of the alcove. He moved with ease, as if he wasn't suffering with arthritis. As if he wasn't eighty-six, but instead a man decades younger.

Later his old Navy SEAL buddies would reminisce about that night and say that their friend looked happier and lighter than they'd seen him in years.

Years later when the alcove was redesigned and a large couch was put in the area so residents could sit and enjoy the sounds and sights of the ocean, people would look up at the medal in the frame on the wall and remember the devotion of the retired Navy SEAL who spent his last years on this planet watching over his wife.

The library was re-named the Caroline Steel Ocean Room.

And every year the people who'd witnessed Matthew "Wolf" Steel's devotion to his wife came together and celebrated the couple's life.

It's said late at night, when the moon is full, that

residents who live at The Establishment will sometimes look out the windows overlooking the boardwalk and see an elderly couple sitting on a bench, holding hands, laughing, as they watched the waves wash up on the beach. But when the residents turn to get a camera, or tell a friend, and look back, the couple has disappeared.

————

If you want to read more about Caroline and Wolf, start with *Protecting Caroline*. You'll see both throughout the SEAL of Protection series...including the last book, *Protecting Dakota* where once again Caroline helps save the day.

THE OTHER SIDE OF THE STORY

by Susan Stoker

AUTHOR NOTE

The Other Side of the Story was written as sort of a prologue to the book, Rescuing Kassie. It explains a little more about why Kassie did what she did in order to meet Hollywood. It can be read before or after Rescuing Kassie.

I just wanted to give the reader a little more insight to Kassie's thinking and why she did what she did.

~Susan

THE OTHER SIDE OF THE STORY

Kassie pulled back her curtain and peeked out, sighing in relief when she didn't see her boyfriend, Richard Jacks. Most of the time when he picked her up, he was late, but today was one day she hoped he didn't show up at all.

It was time to break up with him. He'd changed drastically after he'd gotten back from his latest deployment. An IED had gone off, and while he hadn't been visibly injured, something had to have happened to his brain.

Before deployment, he'd been attentive and fun to be around; now, he was impatient, jealous, and he got angry very easily. Not only that, but he and his best friend, Dean Jennings, had gotten...weird.

When Richard wasn't in Austin, where she lived,

he had Dean follow her around to make sure she wasn't cheating on him. No matter how many times Kassie told Richard that she wasn't seeing anyone but him, he still had Dean keep his eye on her.

It was frustrating, insulting, and downright creepy.

So after tonight's party, she would be telling Richard that things weren't working out between them. She would've done it before now, but they hadn't spent a lot of time with each other recently, and Kassie didn't think it was very cool to break up with someone over the phone.

Richard had also gone to a lot of trouble to set up the party. She didn't want to disappoint him. He'd told her the thing tonight was a kind of Army formal get-together. It was at his apartment, so it wasn't official by any stretch, but he'd said all the guys would be wearing their fancy uniforms and he wanted her to wear a floor-length gown as well.

Kassie didn't know much about Army traditions —okay, she didn't know anything—but she was willing to go along with the party tonight because it seemed to mean a lot to Richard.

Kassie jumped a foot when a knock sounded loud and harsh at her door. She gathered her shawl and purse and took a deep breath before opening the door.

"Hey, Richard. You look very nice."

"You ready?" he asked, not returning the compliment or even thanking her.

Kassie inwardly sighed. She shouldn't spend the evening tallying up all of Richard's faults...but it was hard not to be disappointed that he didn't even mention how she looked. She'd spent quite a while getting ready. She might want to break up with Richard, but she didn't want to embarrass him in front of his friends and the other women who would certainly be there tonight by not looking her best.

"Yeah. I'm ready," she told him, stepping out of her apartment and closing her door. She locked it and when she turned around, Richard was already halfway back to his car. Hesitating for a split second, Kassie seriously thought about unlocking her door and going back inside. Richard already seemed to be in a bad mood, and that certainly didn't bode well for her.

Straightening her shoulders and taking a deep breath, she shook off the feeling of foreboding that sat in her stomach like a piece of undercooked bread. With every breath she took, the ball seemed to grow, millimeter by millimeter.

Kassie shook her head at her silly imagination and followed in Richard's wake. It was a fancy party; how bad could it be?

———

Kassie held on to the cup of water in her hands as if her life depended on it. This was a disaster, and she should've listened to her inner alarm when she stood at her front door. As soon as they'd arrived, Kassie had known the night was going to be Hell on Earth.

First of all, she was the only woman.

Not one of the other men had shown up with a date. If that wasn't bad enough, they were all giving her weird looks out of the corners of their eyes. Richard had invited five others, not including him and Dean. She was outnumbered seven to one. And she wished she'd chosen another dress...maybe even a pantsuit with a high collar and long sleeves.

The navy-blue V-neck sleeveless dress was perfectly appropriate for a fancy party, especially when paired with the shawl she'd brought, but standing in Richard's living room, with his friends eyeballing her cleavage as if they were starving lions who hadn't eaten for months, was more than a little disconcerting.

"Shall we get on with the first Army tradition?" Richard's voice boomed out into the room, scaring the shit out of Kassie. Water sloshed out of the cup she'd been holding and she smiled nervously as the others agreed loudly and boisterously.

"First up is the grog bowl!" Richard announced, and the other men all cheered. Kassie watched as they all gathered around an empty punch bowl. She winced when everyone began pouring the ingredients into the large bowl, which were sitting on the table.

Tomato juice, orange juice, vodka, rum, Jack Daniel's, lemon juice, Tabasco sauce...Kassie blinked and took a sip of the water in her hands, and looked longingly at the door. Maybe she could slip out while everyone was busy.

"...will be my girlfriend."

Kassie jerked when she felt a hand grab her biceps in an unbreakable grip and jerk her toward the table with the punch bowl. She dropped the cup of water she'd been drinking as she tried to pry the man's hand off of her. The others parted around her, giving her room. Richard was standing next to the table with a plastic cup in his hand and a nasty smile on his face.

"The tradition of the grog bowl goes back centuries," he told her. "If someone doesn't answer a question correctly, they have to drink, right guys?"

The men around him all agreed. Kassie made the mistake of meeting Dean's eyes. They were glued to her. His long dark brown greasy hair was pulled back into a ponytail at his nape, and his thin lips were quirked upward in a semblance of a smile. But it was his eyes that caught her attention. They were wide and excited. As if he knew what was about to happen...and couldn't wait.

"So, Kassie, we'll start with you. What year was the Army founded?"

She tore her eyes away from Dean and turned to her boyfriend. "I don't know, I—"

"She doesn't know!" Richard boomed, interrupting her. "Guess that means you have to drink."

Kassie shook her head. "No. That's okay, I don't—"

Her words were cut off when another of Richard's friends moved to her other side and grabbed her arm. The men held her immobile. Her eyes were glued to Richard as she struggled in his friends' grips.

He stepped up to her with the cup of vile liquid and held it out. "Drink, Kassie."

She shook her head frantically. "Richard, I think I need to go."

"No. You need to drink this. It's tradition." He stood there, holding the damn cup out as if it was a glass of champagne and she should be thrilled he'd gotten it for her.

Kassie pressed her lips together. No way in hell was she drinking the disgusting stuff they called grog.

Richard leaned toward her until they were nose to nose, practically touching. She could smell the awful stench of the drink in his hand. "Drink it willingly, or we'll make you. It's tradition. You can't say no."

Tears sprang to her eyes. This definitely wasn't the man she'd begun dating a couple of years ago. She shook her head stubbornly.

Richard stood up to his full height and nodded to someone standing behind her. An arm went around her chest and she couldn't help the surprised screech that came out of her mouth when she was tilted backward.

The men who'd been holding her arms continued to do so as she was hauled to Richard's couch. She was forced to sit between the two men holding her. Richard, still holding the damn cup, straddled her legs, holding her captive under him.

"You didn't answer the question correctly, you have to drink," Richard told her. "You have one more chance to man up and do it on your own."

A tear escaped and Kassie felt it roll down her cheek. "Richard," she whispered...but it didn't affect him in the least. He gave a chin lift to someone behind the couch. A large hand grabbed her chin and wrenched it backward. Her head landed on the cushion behind her and she looked up. Dean was standing there, looking down at her. The evil look in his eyes was intensified now.

"Drink up," Dean murmured, before using his

fingers to press on her jaw. The pain was immediate and Kassie gasped.

Obviously expecting her reaction, Richard brought the cup of grog to her lips and tipped it up.

The vile taste immediately made Kassie gag and she tried to lift her head. Dean pressed harder against her jaw and she felt another hand press down on her forehead.

She struggled in earnest as Richard continued to force the disgusting liquid into her mouth. She kicked out with her legs, and felt someone grab onto her ankles and hold them still. She tried to turn her head, but was held immobile by the hands on her body.

She was well and truly stuck, and her boyfriend was the perpetrator.

Kassie closed her throat, refusing to swallow. The tabasco sauce, along with whatever else they'd thrown into the punch bowl when she wasn't looking, burned the inside of her mouth.

She glared up at Richard, hate filling her soul at what he was doing to her.

"Swallow, Kassie. You didn't answer the question right."

She managed a miniscule shake of her head and Richard smiled.

It was the smile of a man who didn't give a shit

that his girlfriend was crying under him. Who didn't care she was in pain. A smile from a man who had lost whatever decency he'd ever had.

Keeping the cup at her lips, he reached up with his free hand and pinched her nostrils shut.

"You'll drink every drop of this grog, Kassie. You either do it the easy way or the hard way. If you pass out, we'll wait until you come to and we'll start all over again with a full cup."

Kassie struggled as if her life depended on it now. She couldn't breathe. She opened her throat to suck in much needed oxygen and the grog slid down. She choked, and Richard laughed, tipping the cup farther, pouring more of the concoction down her throat. "That's it, baby. Drink it down like a good girl."

Kassie's gag reflex kicked in and her stomach heaved, readying itself to forcibly remove the awfulness that had landed in it.

"If you puke, I'll still make you drink it," Richard threatened.

Kassie closed her eyes and her body went limp. He would, too. He didn't give a shit about her. Whatever had happened in his brain when the IED went off had killed the Richard Jacks she used to know. In his place was an unfeeling bastard whose precious Army traditions meant more to him than anything else.

Knowing she wouldn't be getting up before she finished the fucking cup of grog, Kassie swallowed. Then she did it again. And again. She felt overflow from the awful concoction she couldn't swallow fast enough dripping down her face into her ears. She and prayed Richard would only make her drink this one cup.

She turned off her mind until Richard finally let go of her nose. She sucked in oxygen as if she'd been deprived for hours instead of the thirty seconds of so it had been.

"There now, that wasn't so bad, was it?" Richard crooned to her, leaning down and kissing her lovingly on the lips. Her entire body was still being held in position by his friends, no one had relaxed their grips, and Kassie knew she would bear the marks of their hold for a while to come.

Richard eased off her lap, and whoever was holding her head and legs also released her. Kassie looked up at Dean and he smirked down at her for a moment, running a finger under her bottom lip. "You spilled a bit," he mocked before standing up.

Kassie could feel the grog on her face where it had overflowed from her mouth. She could also feel it on her chest and had no doubt it had soaked into her bra as well.

Richard held out a hand. "Come on, baby. There's

lots more traditions to get through. Aren't Army balls fun?"

She extended her hand, allowing Richard to help her stand upright.

"Why don't you go get cleaned up. Wouldn't want you looking anything less than your best for the receiving line."

The smirk on Richard's face scared Kassie half to death, as did Dean's.

"The receiving line is my *favorite* tradition," he said as she turned to head to the bathroom. She walked toward it on numb legs. She wanted to go home, but Richard had picked her up. She could take a taxi or Uber, but she had a feeling Richard wouldn't let her leave until he'd had *all* his fun.

Kassie shut the bathroom door and leaned over the sink. She stared at herself in the mirror and saw a woman she didn't recognize. Black streaks lined both her cheeks and the side of her face from where her mascara had run when she'd cried. The remnants of the grog were on her lips, chin, neck, in her hair, and disappearing under the vee of her dress onto her chest. Turning her head, Kassie could see the beginnings of a bruise on her jaw from where Dean had held her in his cruel grip.

She was a mess, and Richard had done it to her.

She wanted to be strong enough to march out of

the room and right out the front door, but if she was honest with herself, she was scared.

Richard frightened her.

To death.

She had no idea what he'd do if she tried to leave.

Suddenly, the grog that had been resting uneasily in her belly rebelled. Kassie scrambled for the toilet and made it just in time. If it wasn't bad enough going down, the disgusting liquid was even worse coming back up.

Her nose burned with the alcohol and hot sauce, her throat hurt, and her taste buds were on a permanent strike. Her belly heaved and heaved, and once it had expelled all of the liquid, it kept heaving, as if wanting to get rid of even the *memory* of what had been forced into it.

When she'd finally stopped throwing up, Kassie remained kneeling by the toilet bowl, breathing hard, trying not to break into a thousand pieces.

There was a knock at the door.

"Hurry up, baby. Everyone's waiting for you so we can start the receiving line. I know you're gonna love *this* tradition."

Just the sound of Richard's voice made her stomach heave once more. Kassie took deep breaths and finally got herself under control. She flushed the toilet and stood up, staring at herself in the mirror.

Beyond the mess of her makeup, the bruises on her face, and her lips stained red by the grog, Kassie was disgusted by what she saw.

What had happened to her? How had she gotten to this point? She'd always told her little sister that if someone disrespected her, if they hurt her, to get the fuck out of the situation. And here she was. *Not* getting the fuck out of the situation.

But it was different when it was happening to you.

It was different when you knew your life was in danger if you stood up for yourself.

It was different when one wrong word could make your former boyfriend turn into a monster.

Opening a cabinet, Kassie took out a washcloth and wet it in the sink. She scrubbed her face, ruining the hour of careful work she'd done to make herself up before Richard had arrived. She had no idea what he had planned for the rest of the evening, but she had a bad feeling her night of hell had just started.

"Just do whatever he wants," Kassie said out loud softly, staring at the mirror and the woman she didn't recognize looking back at her. "Get through tonight, then you can break up with him and he'll be out of your life forever. Just because he's a jerk doesn't mean all men are."

With that, Kassie took a deep breath and opened

the bathroom door. Richard was there waiting for her...Dean standing at the end of the hall, watching.

"Ready?" Richard asked, holding out his hand once more.

Kassie nodded.

———

Kassie lie in bed and ignored the peal of her cell phone, knowing it would be her younger sister Karina wanting to know how the thing with Richard went. She was a junior in high school, and Kassie didn't have it in her to talk to her right now. To talk to anyone.

As she'd suspected, her night of hell hadn't ended with that first cup of forced grog. The receiving line was...

Kassie squeezed her eyes closed, trying to force back her tears. She didn't want to think about it anymore. It was over and done.

She curled herself into a tighter ball and pulled her comforter around her.

Two hours later, Kassie woke up once more and reluctantly got out of bed. She couldn't stay there forever, no matter how appealing it might seem.

She showered and pulled on a pair of sweats and a T-shirt. Luckily, she had the day off. The last thing she wanted to do was dress up in a nice outfit and head into JCPenney to try to sell clothes.

Her cell rang again and Kassie saw it was Richard.

And just like that, she was mad. *Furious.* How *dare* he do what he did to her? How dare his friends participate?

Gritting her teeth and deciding right then and there to end things between them, Kassie tapped the button to answer the phone.

"This is Kassie."

"Hey, baby. Good time last night. I was so proud of you."

"It wasn't fun for me, Richard," Kassie told him.

"That's because you weren't sure what to expect. Now that you know the traditions, the next one will be easier. And if I were you, I'd spend some time studying up on the Army...that way you won't have to drink so much grog." Richard laughed at his words, a long cackle that made the hairs on the back of Kassie's neck stand up.

"There's not going to be a next time," she said firmly. "Things aren't working out between us. I think we need to move on."

"What?" Richard asked in a low, even tone that scared the shit of Kassie. If he'd yelled, it would've been different, but that toneless voice was another thing all together.

"You don't even *like* me, Richard. You can't and still do the things you've done to me. Hit me, have me followed. You had your friends hold me down as you forced me to drink that gross stuff."

Silence met her words and Kassie got even more nervous. It should be obvious why she was breaking up with him, but she decided to try a different tactic. One that didn't sound like she was putting the all breakup on him...even though she was. "I mean, you're up there at Fort Hood most of the time, obviously moving up in your Army circles. I'm just holding you back." She tried to sound like she meant it.

"You aren't breaking up with me."

"Richard, I know it's—"

"You don't know shit," he said harshly. "And you *aren't* breaking up with me."

Kassie started to shake. She pulled out one of her kitchen chairs and plopped down into it, her legs like cooked spaghetti.

"You need a woman who can make you proud." She tried to appeal to his arrogant side.

"You're mine, Kassie. You'll always be mine."

"Is that why you let all your friends kiss me last night under the guise of it being an Army receiving line tradition?" She hadn't planned to bring it up, but she couldn't help it. "That's not what boyfriends do." At least, not boyfriends she wanted.

"Is that what's bothering you, baby?" Richard purred. "I shared you with them because I'm proud of you. I want to show everyone what I have. How wonderful you are." As he spoke, his voice gradually changed from sweet and cajoling back to hard and mean. "Besides, you're mine. If I want to watch Dean or anyone else kiss you, or more, I will. And you'll do it. Because I'm the man and I'm in charge."

"Richard, Dean scares me."

"Good. Then you'll do what you're told."

Kassie pressed her lips together. "I'm serious, Richard. I can't do this anymore. I don't want to see you again."

"That's too bad. Because I'm coming over right now and we'll discuss this. I have to go back up to Fort Hood tomorrow. We have a training exercise and we're up against this group of guys who think they're hot shit. We're gonna show them a thing or two. But before I leave, I want to make sure we're solid."

"We're not solid," Kassie protested. "We're broken up."

"No we're not," Richard insisted. "I'll see you soon."

"Richard, don't bother coming over. Richard? Are

you there?" The phone beeped in her ear and Kassie sighed heavily, clicking it off. He'd hung up on her.

Fuck. He was on his way over here. She had to leave. She didn't want to be there when he arrived. She'd just avoid him. They couldn't be boyfriend and girlfriend if they never saw each other, right?

Not knowing how far away Richard was, Kassie ran into her room and threw on a pair of socks and sneakers. She grabbed a hat and pulled it low on her head. The bruises on her arms and legs were hidden by her clothes, but the ones on her face and neck would be harder to disguise for a while.

She ran out of her apartment and locked the door behind her. She quickly walked toward her car and stopped short when she saw Dean leaning against the driver's side.

"Going somewhere, Kassie?"

"Get out of my way, Dean," she said in a tone she hoped was more confident than it sounded to her own ears.

"I don't think so. Richard wants to talk to you, and what he wants, he gets."

"This is crazy," Kassie mumbled.

"It's not. You belong to him, you do what he tells you," Dean informed her, taking hold of her arm in a grip hard enough to hurt...mostly because he grabbed her in the same place she already had bruises from the night before.

He marched her back to her apartment and held on as she unlocked her door. He propelled her in and said, "Make yourself comfortable. Your man will be here soon."

Hating how she meekly did what Dean wanted, Kassie comforted herself with the thought that surely she could talk some sense into Richard when he got there. Who wanted to be with someone who didn't want to be with you right back?

———

A week later, it was getting harder and harder to keep putting Karina off. Her little sister wanted to see her, but with the bruise on her face from where Richard had hit her last week, Kassie refused to. She didn't want Karina to see how bad things had gotten with her big sister and her supposed boyfriend.

When the phone rang, she reluctantly picked it up when she saw it was Richard. She'd definitely learned her lesson and wouldn't risk pissing him off again.

"What?"

"I have a job for you."

Kassie was taken aback for a moment. She'd

thought Richard would apologize for hitting her, would talk about how great the training exercise went that he'd been so looking forward to, even try to sweet talk her and pretend things between them were just fine. "A job?"

"Yeah. There's a dating website you need to sign up for. Then you need to find the profiles of a group of men and message them. Flirt with them, get them interested. Your ultimate goal is to get at least one of them to meet with you, and then find out as much information as you can about them."

"What? Who? What's going on, Richard?" Kassie was confused.

"And before you fucking say it, we are not broken up," he barked out at her. "You're my fucking girl-friend and you're going to fucking do this no matter what."

"Why?"

"Why? You want to know why?"

"Yeah," Kassie whispered, not liking Richard's tone. He sounded exactly like he had in her apartment the week before, when he'd lost it and beaten her.

"Because those fuckers *cheated*. They cheated and embarrassed me and my platoon! They think they're hot shit—and they won't get away with it. I've got plans for them. Oh yeah, big plans."

"Who? Cheated in what?" Kassie asked, still completely lost.

"The fucking exercise!" Richard shouted. "They had us killed before we were even ready to start. They cheated!"

Kassie had no idea what he was talking about, but she tried to placate him anyway. "Okay, Richard. I can do that." She had no intention of trying to lure a guy into talking to her on a website, then using him to give information to Richard. She wouldn't do it. He couldn't *make* her, not like he had with the grog and the other stuff he'd done at his apartment the other night.

"Good. One just started dating a chick with a kid. I can totally use that."

Richard was talking more to himself than to her now, but Kassie didn't interrupt him. She had no idea what he was talking about, but she was scared to death at the implications.

"Yeah. We need a do-over. I can get Dean to help, and my other buddies. We'll need money though...oh yeah, I know just how to get it." He laughed then. An evil laugh that was cold and unfeeling.

"Are you coming to Austin this weekend?" Kassie asked softly, wanting to know if she needed to hide out to stay away from him.

"No. But that doesn't mean you get to fuck

around on me. Dean's there and will keep his eye on you. I gotta go. I'll email you the details." And he hung up without another word.

Kassie clicked off her phone, relieved that Richard wouldn't be coming down to Austin to see her, but feeling nervous for whoever the woman and child were who he'd been mumbling about. That really couldn't be good. She felt a twinge of guilt for feeling glad it wasn't her Richard had set his sights on this time.

Sighing, Kassie went into her bathroom to put on her makeup. She could use a scarf around her neck to hide some of the bruises from her coworkers and the customers, but it looked like she'd need to use a heavier than usual foundation for a while more.

———

Kassie collapsed into her couch and sighed in relief at finally being home. Work was a bitch and it sucked that Dean was still following her around, but at least she hadn't seen Richard in a while.

She clicked on the television and closed her eyes, trying to work up the energy to get up and make something for dinner. The news droned on in the background—and it wasn't until Richard's name was said that she sat up and her eyes popped open in surprise.

Tonight's big story comes from Fort Hood. Sergeant Richard Jacks has been charged with kidnapping and a whole host of other charges stemming from an incident last night. Allegations are that he kidnapped a woman and her child then used them as bait for a platoon of soldiers. Our source tells us that he was upset over a training exercise that took place a couple of months ago and retaliated by kidnapping the girlfriend and child of one of the soldiers he considered responsible for his embarrassment.

Sergeant Jacks was wounded in the altercation, but is expected to survive. He is currently in the hospital and once he recovers, he will stand trial. If convicted, he faces time in federal prison, most likely at Fort Leavenworth in Kansas. Tune in tomorrow morning for the latest updates on the situation.

Kassie tried to suck in breath, but couldn't. Richard had kidnapped the woman and child he'd talked to her about a couple of months ago? He was wounded? He was in *jail*?

For the first time in a long time, almost a year, Kassie felt as if she could breathe.

She was free.

Free of Richard and his threats.

Free of Dean's eyes watching her every move.

She could delete her account at the stupid dating site.

Free.

Her cell phone rang, and Kassie jumped ten feet. She laughed at herself and swiped her thumb across the screen without looking down.

"This is Kassie."

"Don't think you're off the hook."

"What?"

"Don't think you're off the hook," Dean repeated. "Your boyfriend might be behind bars, but nothing changes."

Kassie shook her head in disbelief. "He's not my boyfriend, Dean. This is crazy."

"You're still his woman. Until he tells me differently, I'm keeping my eye on you, as usual. Be a good girl and I won't have to report your defiance to Richard. Step things up on the dating site. Those fuckers think they've beaten us—they haven't. We just need to regroup. And we need intel."

The ball of dread that had disappeared a moment ago was back, tenfold.

"Why are you doing this?"

"Because you belong to Richard. Lock, stock, and barrel. I'll call later with more information."

Kassie stared at her cell phone and collapsed back on the couch. She'd tried to stand up to Dean and Richard. She had. But after her tires had been slashed four times, threatening letters had shown up at work, and Dean himself had shown up at her work time after time, only to stand around and stare at her, she'd caved. It was easier to act like she was going along with what they wanted than to outwardly defy them.

The threat of Richard always loomed over her. He liked to show up at her door and surprise her...and knock her around while he was at it. At least with him behind bars, he couldn't hit her anymore, but Kassie wasn't sure Dean was any less of a threat. He was...creepier. He wouldn't hit her. No, he'd destroy her life however he could—but he wouldn't lay a hand on her.

She took a deep breath and pushed herself up and off the couch. She walked to the table in the other room and clicked on her computer. Might as well get the dating website thing out of the way for the night. With tears in her eyes, she clicked it on and began to search.

Kassie didn't want to make the call, but she had to. She punched in Dean's number on her phone and brought it up to her ear.

"What?"

"I got one of them to answer me."

"Who?"

"Hollywood."

"Good. Now don't fuck it up. We need information. Richard is ready to move this on. He might be behind bars, but he's watching, never forget that."

Kassie felt the resentment well up inside her. "How can I? You tell me every time we talk. I don't like doing this, Dean. I don't know why you guys can't just drop it. Richard is behind bars. It's over. We aren't dating anymore, I haven't seen him in months, this is insane. What is he going to do if I say fuck it? Huh?"

"It's not Richard you need to worry about," Dean said in a low, evil tone. "This fight is our fight for justice. Not just Richard's. You want to know what will happen if you don't do this? If you don't find out what we want to know from one of those assholes? We've been patient. We've been nice about everything. You got cold feet and tried to break up with Richard, but he let it go. But you're still his, Kassie. *His*. His to do with what he wants, when he wants, and with who he wants. But if you need motivation…maybe your sister will give you that incentive."

"What? Karina? What are you talking about? Leave her alone! Please!" Kassie begged.

"You do what you're supposed to, and she'll be fine. Decide to grow a set, and she won't be fine. It's your choice."

"How did I get here?" Kassie whispered more to herself than Dean.

"You're exactly where you're supposed to be," Dean said. "Now, behave yourself and no one will get hurt. Let me know how things are progressing with Hollywood and I'll pass the info on to Richard. As long as you're doing what he told you to do, nothing bad will happen."

Kassie hung up without another word. Through tears, she pulled the keyboard over to her and clicked on the message Hollywood had finally sent her last night. She'd sent him a few messages, not sure he'd ever respond, hoping he wouldn't, but apparently she'd piqued his interest somehow. She closed her eyes and hesitated with her fingers on the keys.

"I'm sorry," she said softly to the man she was messaging, even though he couldn't hear her. "I'm so sorry I'm dragging you into this…but I don't have a choice." Then she took a deep breath, said, "My life sucks," and began to type, returning Hollywood's email and trying to pretend she was a normal girl, trying to meet a man she wanted to date.

———

If you want to find out what happens to Kassie and Hollywood, you can read *Rescuing Kassie*, book 5 in the Delta Force Heroes series.

THE GIFT

by Susan Stoker

AUTHOR NOTE

This short story features little Annie and her new friend, Frankie. You met him in Protecting Kiera. Now, I am aware that PK is only available on Amazon US, but you can read this story and get the gist of who Frankie is and what happened to him in Protecting Kiera.

Also, before you ask...yes I'm planning on writing Annie's story someday. I can't NOT write it. She's an amazing character and I know everyone wants to see her get her HEA.

The question is...will it be with Frankie or not? :)

Enjoy and I hope you get ALL the feels with this story!

-Susan

THE GIFT

ANNIE FIDGETED between her parents and stared hard at the entryway. She squeezed her mom's hand and looked up at her. "How much longer?"

"I don't know, baby," Emily told her daughter. "Their plane landed ten minutes ago, but it sometimes takes a while for everyone to get off. And maybe they had to use the restroom. They'll be here soon. Patience."

"I can't wait to meet Frankie," the little girl told her parents for the millionth time.

Her dad, Cormac "Fletch" Fletcher, squatted down in front of her and put his hands on her shoulders. "Don't be offended if he's shy, squirt," he said. "Since he's deaf, it's probably hard for him to make friends."

Annie nodded enthusiastically. "I know, but I want to show him my Army men, and my room, and where I play cars behind the garage. Do you think he'll want to spend the night with me? There's only one bed in the apartment and the adults will probably want to stay there and even though the couch is super comfy, maybe we can have a sleepover?"

"We'll see," Fletch told her, standing back up. He stepped to his wife's side and leaned in, whispering in her ear, "I'm not sure I'm okay with my daughter setting up sleepovers with boys at age seven."

Emily choked back a laugh and whispered, "We'll see how she feels when she can't communicate with him."

Fletch merely shook his head and grinned. "Don't underestimate our daughter. I think she could make friends with a terrorist if she put her mind to it."

"Isthathimisthathimisthathim?" Annie cried out, jumping up and down in her excitement.

Emily looked up and saw a couple walking toward them. The man was holding the hand of a boy who looked to be about the same age as Annie. When he gave a chin lift to Fletch, she knew for certain it was. "Yes, that's them."

Before the last word was out of her mouth, Annie had taken off running toward the trio. As if they were long-lost brother and sister, she went right up to the little boy and threw her arms around him.

By the time Emily and Fletch had reached the group, Annie had pulled back and was smiling hugely at the boy.

"Coop," Fletch said, holding out his hand. "How was the flight?"

"No problems. Thanks for picking us up."

"Of course. When our commander said you were coming in to give a few classes on using sign language to communicate with others while on missions, I remembered that Tex had talked about you. I couldn't resist the chance to pick your brain before we hit the base."

Cooper "Coop" Nelson chuckled. "I'm always surprised when I run into people who know Tex, but I shouldn't be. This is my girlfriend, Kiera Hamilton."

Fletch shook the woman's hand, as did Emily.

"It's nice to meet you," Emily said. "Fletch said you're a teacher?"

"I am," Kiera said. She also signed the words at the same time. "I work at a school for deaf children. Frankie is one of my students. I met Cooper when he was volunteering there."

"And his dad let you fly him across the country?" Emily asked, her eyebrows raised in surprise.

"Yeah. We went through a...thing," Kiera looked over at Cooper and shrugged, then continued, "He kinda made us Frankie's God-parents and we're all pretty close."

Fletch wanted to know more about the "thing" Kiera mentioned, but figured he'd ask Cooper later. He felt a tug on his shirt and looked down at Annie. He and Emily had taught her that it was rude to interrupt, but sometimes her enthusiasm got the better of her. "I wanna tell Frankie my name with my fingers. But I don't know how."

Kiera squatted down next to the children. She patiently showed Annie how to finger spell her name for Frankie. She caught on quickly. She turned to the little boy, who had stayed glued to Cooper's side, and waved her little hand, pointing to herself, then painstakingly spelled out A-N-N-I-E.

A smile came across the boy's face for the first time. He waved back, pointed to himself, then spelled his own name.

Without a word, Annie tried to copy him, and when she forgot one of the letters, Frankie reached out and helped her manipulate her fingers and hand into making the letter.

Kiera stood up and smiled at Cooper. "Looks like they're going to get along just fine."

They all headed down the escalator toward the baggage claim area, chatting about nothing in particular. Cooper and Fletch talked about work, Emily and Kiera made small talk about the apartment over the garage where they'd be staying, and what Kiera might want to do while Cooper was at the base working, and Annie and Frankie gestured back and forth, giggled, and solidified their fast friendship.

———

Emily sat with Kiera on the back patio after dinner and after the men had disappeared inside to talk shop. The two women watched Annie and Frankie playing together in the grass. Annie had brought out her precious Army men Fletch had given her when he'd first met her. They were still in their boxes, even though the cardboard was looking a little rough around the edges. All around the Barbie-size dolls were little plastic green Army men, matchbox cars, and little metal tanks she'd gotten for Christmas the year before.

The two kids were playing happily, communicating by gesturing back and forth and lots of pointing.

"What's Frankie's story?" Emily asked.

"He was sick when he was a baby and lost his hearing. His dad moved to our area and enrolled Frankie in my school. He was withdrawn and sullen because of the drama and upheaval of the move and his discontent at his home life. It didn't help that his mom made it clear she didn't really like her son and the fact that he couldn't hear."

Emily sucked in a horrified breath. "Oh my God. Poor Frankie."

"Yeah, I'm super over-simplifying here, but his dad divorced the woman, partly because she was a bitch and mostly because she was a freaking drug addict. Frankie met Cooper, who in no way could ever be called anything less than a man, and immediately got a case of hero-worship...not that I can blame him."

"Well, thank God for that," Emily said, sitting back in her chair in relief.

"Oh, but then she came to the school and tried to kidnap him."

Emily's eyes opened so wide, they looked like they'd bug right out of her head.

Kiera laughed. "Don't worry. I jumped in her car too and Cooper and one of his friends came to our rescue. But Frankie learned firsthand that day how cool it was to be able to speak in secret code." Kiera held up her hands and made air quotes around the last two words.

Emily smiled at her. "And you? How'd you learn sign language?"

"My mom is deaf."

"Ah. Makes sense. So Frankie's dad was okay with you guys bringing him with you to Texas?"

"Yeah. After the attempted kidnapping, and with Cooper rescuing his son and me putting myself in danger for him, he officially made us Frankie's God-parents His dad had an out-of-town meeting and we volunteered to bring Frankie with us."

"That's amazing. I know I trust any of Fletch's friends with Annie's life," Emily said.

The little girl laughed just then, and the two adults turned to see what was so funny.

Annie was giggling so hard, she'd fallen onto her back in the grass and was rolling around in glee.

"What's so funny?" Emily called out.

Annie turned on her side and propped her head up with a hand as she looked over at her mom. "Frankie is. He's hilarious."

Emily looked confused. "But you guys can't talk to each other," she informed her daughter.

Annie sat up and scooted over to Frankie and threw her arm over his shoulders before saying, "We can so. He just told me a joke."

"He did?" Emily asked, tilting her head in confusion.

"Yeah," Annie confirmed. "He said, 'Why did the Army man cross the road?'"

When the little girl didn't continue, Emily asked, "Why?"

"He was protecting the chicken," Annie said, then burst into giggles all over again.

The adults looked at each other for a long moment before grinning. It wasn't *that* funny, but they'd both learned a long time ago that what was funny to a seven-year-old wasn't necessarily a laugh-riot to everyone else.

Annie and Frankie went back to their playing, occasional bouts of laughter from Annie ringing out over the lawn. An hour later, Cooper and Fletch came back outside and Kiera signed to Frankie that it was time for bed.

"Please, can Frankie have a sleepover?" Annie asked before they left.

"Not tonight," Emily told her. "He's most likely tired from traveling and the last thing he needs is to be kept awake by an excited little girl."

"But, Mommmmm," Annie pouted.

"Your mom said no," Fletch said sternly. "If you're good, and if he wants to, we'll discuss it with Cooper and Kiera for tomorrow night."

As if her dad had already said yes, Annie's face brightened and she waved at Frankie.

He signed something to her and before anyone could translate, Annie had copied the sign.

Frankie smiled and repeated it one more time, then waved.

After the trio had left to walk across the yard to the garage apartment where they'd be staying, Emily asked her daughter, "How did you know what Frankie was saying to you?"

Annie shrugged. "I figured it out."

"But how?"

"I don't know, Mom, it just made sense. I waved at him, and I remember him telling Miss Kiera his dinner was good, and she translated what he was saying at dinner, remember? Anyway, so the first thing he said was good, and I figured the other was night."

Emily stared at her daughter. She was right. She hadn't remembered the conversation at dinner, but Annie never missed much, never had.

"I love you," Emily said.

"I love you too," Annie replied, then spun and ran for the dining room table, where she'd laid out her precious Army men after coming inside. She gathered them into her arms and raced past her parents and toward her room.

SUSAN STOKER

"Fifteen minutes, squirt," Fletch called after her.

"Okay, Daddy!" Annie yelled back, but didn't slow down.

Emily shook her head and turned into her husband. "Are we sure we want another Annie around here?"

Fletch put his hands on his wife's ass and pulled her into him. "Absolutely. There's nothing I can think of that would please me more than to have more little yous running around."

Emily grinned, feeling her husband's erection against her belly. "Maybe I'll go take a bath while you put our daughter to bed."

Fletch groaned. "The image of you naked in our tub isn't going to make this erection I have go down anytime soon."

"After you put Annie to bed, I'll take care of that for you," Emily told him, her lips twitching. "You know this is my fertile time of the month."

"You are evil," Fletch said, squinting at her. "You know when she's worked up it takes twice as long to get her settled."

"I'll just have to get started without you then," Emily said.

With that, Fletch pulled her into him and kissed her with all the pent-up passion her teasing had generated. Pulling away several minutes later, he turned Emily and pushed her toward the hall. "Go. I need a couple minutes to control myself before I go to Annie."

Emily stepped away, swaying her hips in an exaggerated movement as she went. Looking over her shoulder, she smiled at Fletch. "See you in bed, honey."

———

One of Fletch's favorite times of the day was his bedtime routine with Annie. He wasn't always home in the evenings to share the time with her, but when he was, he treasured their conversations. Sometimes they talked about nothing important, other times Annie shared her fears with him, but tonight she was, not surprisingly, interested in talking about Frankie.

"How did he lose his hearing?"

"He was sick as a baby and the infection broke his ears."

"How did he learn to sign?"

"I suppose the same way you learned to talk."

"Can I learn to sign?"

"Yeah, squirt, I'm sure you can. You were already signing with him today."

"I want to talk more with him. I like him."

"I think he likes you too. I'm sure he'd like to be able to talk to you."

"But how can I talk to him if he can't hear me on the phone?"

"You can talk to him on the phone, Annie. It's a special phone; when you talk, it types out what you're saying to him."

"But how does he talk back to me if he doesn't use words?"

Fletch paused at that. "I'm not sure." He tried to always be honest with Annie.

His daughter looked distressed, then her bottom lip wobbled. "But he's going to go home in a couple of days and I won't be able to talk to himmmm."

The last word was wailed as she began to cry.

"Shhhh, baby. We'll talk to Cooper and Kiera and see if they can help us. I'm sure they know more about it than I do."

Annie continued to sniff, and her tears continued to fall down her little cheeks.

"Come here, baby," Fletch said, and got her settled under her covers. He lay down and rested his head on the pillow next to her. She was on her back and he was on his side. "I was proud of you today."

"W-w-why?"

"Because I'm sure some kids aren't nice to Frankie because he can't hear them."

"That's dumb. He's funny."

Fletch smiled. "He is. But some people don't take the time to try to get know people who are different from them."

"He likes my Army men," Annie told him.

The smile on Fletch's face didn't dim. Liking Annie's precious Army men was one way she decided if someone was worth her effort. And apparently, Frankie had passed her test. "I saw that."

"If I could, I'd sell my Army men to buy us a way to talk to each other when he's a million miles away."

Fletch blinked. He could only recall one other time Annie had offered to sell her precious toys—that was when her mom was in desperate need of money and hadn't been eating. She took the plastic dolls everywhere with her. She refused to open the boxes, saying it would make them "old." The fact that she'd voiced out loud the desire to sell them for a little boy she'd been around for only a few hours, who she wanted to keep in touch with, was surprising. And all Annie.

"I don't think that'll be necessary, squirt. I'll talk to Miss Kiera and Cooper and see what they think, okay?"

"Tomorrow?"

"Yeah, tomorrow."

"Okay. Can we go online to Mazon and order a book to help teach me to talk with my hands?"

"Amazon?"

"Yeah, that's what I said."

Fletch nodded his head. "Yeah, I think we can do that."

Annie turned on her side and mirrored her dad's position with one hand under her head. Her little cheeks were still flushed and she sniffed once before saying, "I'm gonna marry him, daddy."

"You are, huh?"

"Yeah. And I need to learn how to talk to him as soon as possible. It wouldn't be good if I couldn't talk to or understand my husband, would it?"

Fletch wanted to protest, but he'd learned from Emily, and from being around Annie, that the more he argued against something, the more Annie seemed to want it. She'd grow out of it, she was only seven. "No, you're right. It'd be good if you could talk to your husband."

Annie nodded. "Okay. You won't forget to talk to Miss Kiera about it?"

"No, I won't forget."

"Good. Now go, Daddy."

"Go? You don't want me to read to you tonight?"

Annie shook her head. "Nope. I'm tired and I want my brain to rest so I can learn as much as I can tomorrow about how to talk with my hands. I want to learn the alphabet tomorrow."

"Okay, squirt. You sleep well." He stood up, then leaned over and kissed Annie on her forehead.

Annie looked up at him and signed "good night," as she'd learned from Frankie earlier.

Fletch smiled and returned the sign.

Smiling happily, Annie closed her eyes and snuggled down into her pillow.

Later that night, much later, after Fletch had made love to his wife, thoroughly and with quite a lot of vigor, he informed her of their daughter's upcoming nuptials.

"You didn't disagree with her or tell her she'd change her mind later, did you?" Emily asked sleepily, not in the least concerned about her daughter's pronouncement.

"Hell no. I've learned that lesson."

"She'll probably tire of him by the end of the weekend," Emily predicted. "You know how she is."

Fletch did know how his daughter was. He didn't voice his opinion, but he had a feeling a weekend with the little boy wasn't going to dampen Annie's enthusiasm one bit.

"I'm sure. Sleep, sweetheart," he ordered Emily.

"You're so bossy," she mumbled, but she pulled Fletch's hand, which was wrapped around her chest, up to her lips and kissed the palm. "I kinda like this trying-to-get-pregnant thing," she told him.

He smiled. "Me too. But even if it never happens, or it takes five years, I'll never stop loving you. In fact, with every day that goes by, I love you more."

"The feeling is definitely mutual. But I have a hunch it's not going to take years. If your sperm is half as bossy as you are, it's only a matter of time."

Fletch smiled. Giving his sperm anthropomorphic qualities was such an Emily thing to do.

"Good night."

"Night," Emily replied.

———

"Did you have a good time with Annie today?" Kiera signed to Frankie.

"Yes!" the little boy enthusiastically signed back. "She's nice."

"You seemed to get along with her just as good or better than Jenny and the other girls in our class," she told him.

Frankie shrugged. "She's different."

"Different how? Because she doesn't know sign language?" Kiera asked.

"No. Because I love her."

Kiera looked down at Frankie in shock. Cooper

had already said good night to the little boy and was currently in the bedroom, getting ready for bed. She'd wanted to reassure herself that Frankie was doing okay. He didn't travel much, and being around people who could hear could be exhausting and confusing for him. The last thing Kiera expected was for him to declare his love for the little girl in the house across the yard.

"You do, huh?"

Frankie nodded. "She thinks I'm funny and she shared her special toys with me. She doesn't care that I sound funny when I laugh or try to talk, and she tried really hard to learn some signs today. I love her."

Kiera smiled and did her best not to look skeptical or to laugh. The mind of a child was a wonderful and strange thing. "Well, tomorrow you can get to know her more. Does that sound good? You want to spend the day with her and her mom while Cooper and her dad do business on the Army post?"

Frankie's head bobbed up and down enthusiastically. "I want to get her a present," he told Kiera.

"A present?"

"Yes. Something she can remember me by so she doesn't decide she loves someone else and forget about me before I can grow up and come back for her."

Kiera felt her heart melting. "What kind of

present?" She knew he didn't have any money with him, but it didn't matter, she'd pay for whatever trinket he wanted to get for his crush.

"I don't know yet. But I'm sure when I get to know her better tomorrow, I'll figure it out. How many more days do we have here?"

"Two full days, then we fly back home on the third."

His bottom lip stuck out in a pout as he signed, "That's not long enough."

"I'm sure you guys can keep in touch after you go home," Kiera tried to reassure him.

He shrugged. "I'll think of something to get her so she can't forget me. Something that every time she looks at it, she remembers me."

"I know you will. Now it's time for sleep. Close your eyes, we'll have more fun tomorrow."

"Thanks for talking my dad into letting me come with you, Miss Kiera. This is the best thing I've ever done in my life."

She leaned over and kissed him on the top of the head before signing, "You're welcome. Good night."

"Good night. Did you see how fast Annie picked up on how to say good night? I only signed it once and she knew what it meant."

"I saw. Now hush. Go to sleep," Kiera ordered.

Frankie nodded and turned on his side on the couch.

She turned out the lights and headed into the small bedroom where Cooper was waiting for her. She climbed into the bed and snuggled into the large man, feeling at home with him no matter where they were bedded down.

"He tell you he's in love with Annie?" Cooper asked.

Kiera lifted her head and stared at her boyfriend. "How'd you know?"

"Because that was the first thing he wanted to talk to me about when you left the room. When did I know you were the woman for me."

"And what did you tell him?" Kiera asked.

"The second I laid eyes on you, I knew you would change my life."

"And?" she inquired.

"And Frankie nodded, and said it was the same with him. That the second Annie hugged him in the airport, he knew he loved her."

Kiera stared at Cooper for a long moment before asking, "You don't really believe him, do you?"

"Weirder things have happened," he responded.

Settling back into his side, Kiera said, "He's only seven and lives on the other side of the country. He'll forget about her as soon as he gets back and little Jenny bats her eyelashes at him again."

"Hmmmmm."

From the few months they'd been dating, Kiera knew that sound meant he neither agreed nor disagreed with her. She decided to blow it off. It didn't really matter one way or the other. They would be leaving with Frankie in another two days. Annie would be out of his life and that would be that.

———

The next night, after dinner, Frankie pulled Kiera aside.

"Are you okay, Frankie?" she signed, looking over at the Fletchers. Emily and Fletch were sitting on the couch and Annie was on the floor. She had her Army men propped up against the legs of the coffee table and she and Frankie had been paying some sort of convoluted game Kiera hadn't been able to make heads nor tails of. But it didn't matter, as the two children seemed to be happy as clams.

The day had started out with breakfast in the big house. Afterward, Cooper and Fletch had gone off to the post for the training class Cooper was giving on the importance of a universal hand signal program for soldiers.

Emily and Kiera had taken the kids to Mayborn Museum. There were over a dozen rooms for children, and Annie and Frankie had spent several hours being entertained. There were a few awkward moments when other children were pointing and whispering about Frankie behind his back, but Annie had stood up for him and told the kids flat out they were being rude, and if they thought something was wrong with Frankie simply because he couldn't hear, *they* were the stupid ones.

Emily had scolded her daughter for her harsh words, but they'd seemed to work. After that, the ice had been broken and they'd all played together.

Then they'd gone to a mall in Temple, simply to kill some time. They'd stopped and talked to a woman named Kassie who worked in JCPenney, and who was the girlfriend of one of Fletch's teammates. They'd grabbed a snack at the food court and had walked around.

At one point, Kiera had looked down at the kids and nudged Emily. Frankie and Annie were holding hands. Frankie was signing with his free right hand and Annie was attempting to spell out words with her left as they walked.

It was as cute as anything she'd ever seen. As they'd watched, a man bumped into Annie, who stumbled and would've fallen if it hadn't been for

Frankie holding on to her. He immediately dropped Annie's hand and took a step in front of her. Kiera gasped as she watched Frankie's lightning fast hand movements as he tore into the man for not watching where he was going and for almost hurting Annie.

The man had looked at Kiera and shrugged.

"He says that you could've hurt Annie," Kiera told the man, taking the liberty of paraphrasing so as not to get into an altercation right there at the mall. Frankie was mad. It was clear to see.

"Sorry, little dude," the man mumbled, then turned his back and walked away, even though Frankie was still "talking" to him.

It took a moment for Kiera to calm Frankie down enough for them to continue their stroll around the mall. It wasn't until Annie herself took Frankie's hand back in her own and smiled at him to let him know she was all right that he finally calmed down enough to continue.

Now they were home, fed, and relaxed...at least Kiera had thought they were all relaxed.

"I know what I want to get Annie," the little boy signed.

"What?"

"Doll cases for her Army men," Frankie told her. "The boxes hers are in are falling apart, and she told me she was worried that if they broke, her soldiers would be ruined," he explained. "I saw some when we were walking around today."

Kiera frowned for a moment, then signed, "They're probably really expensive." From what she could tell, Annie's dolls probably cost at the most about ten bucks. Spending fifty dollars or more per case in order to keep cheap toys safe seemed silly to her.

"So?" Frankie signed impatiently.

"What if you got her new Army men?" Kiera suggested.

Frankie shook his head stubbornly. "No. She loves the ones she has. Fletch gave them to her. I want to protect those for her."

"I'm not sure your dad will approve of spending that much money on someone you just met," Kiera told Frankie slowly. "Maybe you can think of something less expensive."

"I'll pay for them," the little boy told her, his little lips drawn together in a tight line of concentration.

"Do you have that much money?" Kiera asked.

"Not right now, but I can earn it. I'll do jobs around the house. I can ask dad if there's something I can do to earn money. I don't care how long it takes, even if I never get an allowance until I'm really old, like thirteen, I'll do it."

Kiera tried not to smile at that. Really old at thirteen. Being around kids certainly made her feel ancient sometimes. "What if your dad doesn't have that much money to loan you?"

Frankie's shoulders slumped. It was obvious he hadn't thought about that. His eyes wandered around the room as he tried to figure out a solution in his head. Kiera saw him stare at Annie for a long moment before he turned around and said, "Tell my daddy I'll sell the iPad I got for Christmas to pay for it."

Kiera stared at Frankie in shock. He *loved* that iPad. He'd talked about it nonstop in the talk circle in the classroom. Had said that with an app he had on there, he could actually "talk" to hearing people. He'd said it gave him a sense of freedom and more confidence to go out into the hearing world on his own. For him to tell her he'd sell it to buy something for Annie was shocking.

"I'm sure he wouldn't want you to do that, what about—"

Frankie interrupted her and shook his head, his light brown hair flying around his head. "No. It'll be enough to buy the cases, right? The good ones? Not the cheap ones?"

Kiera slowly nodded. "I'm sure it will be."

"You'll call him tonight, tell him?"

"You could call him and use the built-in camera and the app to tell him yourself," Kiera said.

Frankie shook his head again. "No. I'll be busy with Annie. She said I could spend the night and we're gonna make a tent city and obstacle course in her room. I won't have time."

"Okay, Frankie. If you're sure it's what you want."

"I'm sure," he signed. Looking over at Annie once more, he met Kiera's gaze. "She's worth it. Even if I can't see her on my special app and can only email her until I can make enough money to afford to buy a new iPad, she's worth it."

And with that, the little boy went right back to Annie's side and they began playing as if he hadn't been gone.

Kiera went back and sat next to Cooper and he asked, "Everything okay?"

"It's good. I'll talk to you later."

Looking concerned, but realizing it wasn't an emergency, Cooper nodded and they all went back to watching the movie.

———

An hour later, Emily was helping Annie get ready for bed while Fletch was assisting Frankie.

"I know you want to play more, but only another hour. I mean it, Annie. I'll be checking on you guys. You need to get some sleep for another fun day tomorrow."

"Okay. Mommy?"

"Yes, baby?"

"Will you talk to daddy and have him go to the store tomorrow and buy the present we talked about for Frankie?"

Emily sighed. She'd hoped her daughter would've forgotten about this with the excitement of the day and with Frankie sleeping over. "We'll see."

Annie's face scrunched up in what Emily recognized as a precursor to a monster of an argument. "I talked to Kiera today. She said that there's a special camera thing that's been put on sale recently that hooks into a 'puter or iPad and not only shows someone's picture and lets the other person hear what they're saying, but it has a little computerized person that puts what is said into sign language in a little box in the corner. It's like FaceTiming, but it translates."

Emily stared at Annie in shock. She knew Annie wanted to talk to Frankie when he left, but assumed she wanted something like a web camera or something. That was cheap...and easy. "If it's a special thing, I'm not sure we can just go into a store and buy it, sweetie."

"True," Annie said, sounding no less determined

or put off. "But Kiera said they had them out in California in special stores. We could order it and Frankie could pick it up when he gets home."

"Why don't you start out with writing him letters, then if he wants to continue, we can look into a webcam."

"No. I'm going to learn sign language and Frankie is going to help me. He can't do that if we can't see and talk to each other."

Emily sighed and sat on the side of Annie's bed. "It sounds expensive, honey."

"I know," Annie said and wrinkled her nose. "I asked Miss Kiera how much and she wasn't sure. But, Mommy, I have something that's worth a *lot* of money."

"What's that?"

"My Army men."

Emily sucked in a breath. Annie had mentioned selling her precious Army men the night before, but she'd thought her daughter had just been talking. As she continued to press her case, Emily realized that whatever it was Annie felt toward Frankie was serious.

"I know they're worth a lot a *lot* of money. They're still in their boxes and brand new. 'Member when I told you to sell them when we were poor and Daddy Fletch wasn't in our life? You said they were worth a lot and I should keep them until a time when I found something I really wanted. Well, I *really* want this."

Climbing into Emily's lap, Annie turned huge eyes up to her mom. She wound her arms around her mom's neck and looked right into her eyes. "I don't want Frankie to go back to California and forget about me. I want to be able to ask how his day went. I want to celebrate his birfdays with him and if any other girl thinks he's hers, I want to tell him that isn't the case. Please, Mommy? I know if Daddy takes them to the pawn shop, he'll get a ton of money for them and then I can afford to get Frankie this special camera thingy."

Emily sighed. Annie wasn't a child who asked for much. She never had been. There was no way she could deny her this. Especially when it wasn't something Annie wanted for herself. If she was willing to sell her most prized possessions, who was she to stand in her way? Emily knew the toys would only bring in about ten dollars, if that, but between her and Fletch, they could afford to make up the difference and purchase the special equipment.

"Okay, baby. I'll get your dad to take your toys to the pawn shop tomorrow and call Frankie's dad and make arrangements for the camera. Are you sure about this? Once your Army men are gone, we won't be able to get them back."

"I'm sure," Annie said immediately, a smile on her face from ear to ear. "I'll miss them, but I'll get to talk to Frankie every day in return. It'll be worth it. Can you get his dad to email a picture of the special camera? I want to print it out and give it to him tomorrow as a present before he leaves."

"Yeah, I'm sure we can arrange that."

"He's gonna be so surprised! I can't wait to see his face," Annie said.

Just then, Fletch knocked on the door. "Permission to enter?" he asked. Frankie was by his side, smiling at Annie.

In a flash, Annie leaped off her mom's lap and was in front of Frankie. She gestured for him to follow her, not that he had a choice, as Annie had latched onto his hand and was dragging him over to a pile of blankets and towels they'd brought in earlier in preparation for making their "tent city."

"I guess we're forgotten," Fletch said, putting his arm around Emily's waist. "Did you have a good talk?"

"Just wait until I tell you what you're doing tomorrow," Emily told Fletch with a rueful shake of her head.

"That bad?" Fletch asked, leading her out of their daughter's room.

"Not bad, but surprising for sure," she said.

———

The next night, the last night Annie and Frankie would be together for a long time, the adults sat at the table in the dining room while the children went into the family room. Annie had asked for some privacy while she "talked" with Frankie.

"Are you sure you don't want me there to translate?" Kiera had asked the little girl.

Annie had shaken her head and said, "I can understand him just fine."

The adults had shrugged. They didn't know if Annie was being one hundred percent honest, but they all loved her attitude.

When the kids had disappeared into the other room, Kiera leaned across the table and asked Emily, "What did Annie get for Frankie? I think it's so cute they each wanted to get something for the other."

"I know, right?" Emily said with a chuckle. "Thanks to your discussion with Annie, she decided she had to get that special camera thing. You know, the one that has the little human figure in the corner that translates spoken word into sign language. Frankie's dad is picking it up today and will have it at the airport when you guys get home tomorrow."

"What?" Kiera said, clearly taken aback.

"I know, I know, it's expensive, but Annie insisted. Even had Fletch sell her Army men to pay for it." Emily chuckled. "As if that would cover it, but it honestly wasn't as expensive as I thought it would be. Frankie can plug the little camera into his iPad and download the app and Annie can use her regular camera and download the app. They'll be able to talk as much as they want. I know it'll help Annie learn sign language too."

"She sold her Army men?" Kiera asked.

"Yup."

"Holy cow."

"Ask me what Frankie got for Annie," Kiera told Emily.

"I'm almost scared to ask," she said.

"An expensive pair of cases for her Army men," Kiera said matter-of-factly.

Emily's eyes widened in her face. "He didn't."

"Now ask where he got the money to pay for them."

"No...please don't say his iPad," Emily breathed.

"Yup. His precious iPad, which he's usually glued to. He wanted to get the most expensive and best-built plastic cases, so Annie wouldn't have to worry about her Army men getting dirty or 'used'."

"Holy crap. We're in the middle of a *Gift of the Magi* story," Emily breathed.

Neither said anything for a heartbeat, until Kiera whispered, "I need to see this play out."

Apparently in agreement, Emily followed Kiera as she tiptoed to the door of the family room. Fletch and Cooper met them there and they all watched as the two kids exchanged gifts.

———

Annie was so excited to give Frankie his gift. It looked really small next to the two large boxes he had wrapped up for her, but it didn't matter. He was going to love it.

Smiling at him, she handed him the envelope with the picture of the fancy camera that would translate her words into sign language for him. He'd told her the first day they'd met how much he loved his iPad and how much he used it. This was perfect.

She was still grinning at him as he unwrapped it. He pulled the picture out of the envelope and stared at it for the longest time.

Too excited to wait, she grabbed it out of his hand and pointed to it. Then she pointed to herself and to him. Then brought her hand up to her ear, pantomiming a phone, then she made some fake signs with her hand and pointed at him. Then down at the picture she was holding. Then back to herself.

Annie grinned huge and handed the picture back to him, extremely pleased with herself.

Frankie didn't smile. In fact, he barely moved, just continued to stare down at the picture of the fancy camera for the deaf.

Finally, he gave her a small smile, and put the picture down. Then he pushed the two big boxes over to Annie.

Confused now, and a little worried that it didn't seem like Frankie was all that excited about talking with her once he left, Annie tore the paper off the first box. She saw the picture on the box—and her smile faded. She turned to the next present and opened it just as quickly. It was a duplicate of what was in the first box. She looked up at Frankie.

He was smiling at her. He made the sign for man, and then soldier—he'd taught those to her the first time she'd shown him her Army men—then pointed to the boxes. He nodded and his eyebrows went up as if to say, cool huh?

He pointed at her, then made a gesture as if to ask, where are they?

Annie stared at the beautiful cases for her Army men. Frankie had gone out of his way to get her something he knew she'd love. She felt a pang of sorrow for the toys she knew were gone forever, but bravely smiled through it.

Frankie had to care about her. He wouldn't have gotten her something so expensive if he didn't. He never had to know she'd sold her toys to give them the ability to talk to each other.

Pointing to her dad's iPad sitting on the table, she pointed at it, then to Frankie. She gestured toward the door, hoping he'd understand that she wanted him to go get his own device so they could download the app and get familiar with it so they could talk when he got home.

When he didn't move, Kiera wiggled in her seat. They simply stared at each other, as if waiting for the other to make a move.

———

"Can I interrupt? Kiera asked from the doorway.

Annie jumped in surprise, then touched Frankie on the arm to get his attention and pointed at Kiera.

Annie nodded.

Kiera and Emily filed into the room, while Fletch and Cooper stayed near the doorway.

"Do you like your present?" Kiera signed to Annie.

She nodded and signed, "Yes." Then she turned to Frankie and said, "I love it, Frankie. It's perfect."

Frankie's hands moved then, signing quickly, as if

he was excited about something. Kiera translated as he spoke. "I knew you'd love them. They're perfect for your soldiers. They'll stay the same and perfect for you forever. You don't have to worry about the boxes breaking anymore. Go get them. I want to make sure they fit."

"What about you, Frankie?" Kiera asked. "Do you like your present from Annie?"

"Yeah, it's great," he signed a little less enthusiastically.

"It's so we can talk when you go home," Annie said softly. "I really like you and would like to learn sign language so we can use regular cameras to talk, but until then, this will translate what I'm saying and what you're saying back to me. The little computer person in the corner will make the signs as we talk. You plug the camera into your iPad on your end and I just need the app on mine. I'm sure Daddy Fletch or Cooper will help us set it up if you go get your iPad."

The kids stared at each other for a long moment before Emily put her hand on her daughter's shoulder and said, "Sweetie, Frankie sold his iPad to pay for the cases for your Army men."

Annie stared at Frankie with wide eyes. "He did?"

"Yeah."

"But I sold my Army men to pay for the special

camera thing," she said, not taking her eyes off Frankie's face.

The second Kiera finished translating for her, Frankie's gaze whipped back to Annie's. He tilted his head and spelled out slowly, "You did?"

Annie nodded.

The adults all held their breath, waiting for a reaction from the children. They were going to be upset, that was for sure. They'd each sold one of the most important possessions they had to get something for the other, and now both presents were essentially useless.

It was Annie who broke first.

A giggle erupted from her throat. She covered her mouth with her hand to try to stifle it, but it was no use. Another escaped, then another. Before long, the little girl was laughing hysterically.

And amazingly, Frankie had joined in. They'd fallen backwards and were rolling around on the floor laughing as if they'd never stop.

"Huh," Cooper exclaimed over the din. "Didn't expect *that* reaction." He then turned to Fletch. "Think we should bring out *our* presents now?"

Fletch nodded, and the two men strode all the way into the room, each with a present in their arms. Cooper handed a small box to Frankie and Fletch handed a larger box to his daughter.

Cooper signed to Frankie as Fletch spoke.

"I know you guys are probably a little disappointed with your gifts, but—"

"Daddy," Annie interrupted. "I love my gift. Yeah, I'm a little sad I don't have my Army men to put inside them, but Frankie got them for me. And he did it because he likes me and wanted me to be happy. I can't be too sad."

"Me too," Frankie signed. "I'm glad Annie wants to talk to me after I leave. Because I want to talk to her too. I'll do extra chores and earn enough money to get a new iPad, then we can talk."

"Well," Fletch said, "I'm glad you guys aren't mad at each other. Go ahead and open your presents from us now."

Both kids tore into their gifts—and their little gasps of disbelief rang out in the room.

Annie lifted her two Army men from her box at the same time Frankie pulled out his beloved iPad. Two sets of eyes whipped up to the men.

"How?" Annie asked.

At the same time, Frankie signed, "How did you get this?"

Fletch smiled. "Emily told me what Annie wanted to get for you, Frankie, and Kiera told Cooper what you were supposed to get for Annie. Then it was simply a matter of me and Cooper talking. I can't tell you how proud we are of both of you. The fact that you like each other enough to want to get each other a gift is great. But it's even more amazing that you were each willing to sell something you loved in order to get the other something you thought they would enjoy is amazing. *You two* are amazing. We couldn't bear to sell your things. Now you can both enjoy the gifts you were given."

Annie jumped up off the floor and gave her dad a hug. Then she hugged Cooper. Not wanting the women to feel left out, she hugged both her mom and Kiera. Then she turned to Frankie and threw her arms around him too.

The two children stood in the middle of the room with their arms around each other, and Emily looked up to her husband.

"Remember this moment," she said softly. "I have a feeling at some point in our lives, we'll be watching them hug just like this at their wedding."

Fletch strolled across the room and sat on the couch next to his wife. As Annie and Frankie turned their attention to her Army men and how to open the protective cases to insert the battered boxes, he said, "If an adult Frankie can do what it takes to make an adult Annie as happy as she is right this minute, I have no problem with it."

———

The next day, Frankie sat in his seat on the plane with a large plastic box in his lap. Annie had given him one of her precious Army men, saying he could keep it safe for her and they could play with them again when they next saw each other.

"Happy, Frankie?" Kiera signed when they were settled.

He nodded. Then he turned to his other side and asked Cooper, "How old do I have to be to get married?"

"Eighteen, buddy."

"That's a long time from now," Frankie mused.

"It is and it isn't," Cooper told the little boy. "It doesn't matter if she's eighteen or forty-eight. You wait until the time is right. She might want to go to college, or fly to the moon, and you let her. Just let her know that you're right there beside her, cheering her on, whether you're literally right beside her or thousands of miles across the country. When the time is right for you to claim your woman, you'll know it."

Frankie looked up at the man he admired above almost all other men...except for his dad, of course. "What if she doesn't want me?"

Cooper tapped the box in Frankie's arms. "She

wants you, buddy. Be a man she can rely on. Who she can call when she's sad or happy. Support her. Love her. And she'll eventually come to you."

"Promise?"

"Promise."

"You can't promise that," Kiera said from behind Frankie. "Don't set him up for heartbreak."

When Frankie nodded and looked down at the picture of the special camera Annie had arranged for him to have, Cooper looked at the love of his life.

"If I had met you when I was a kid, I would've done whatever it took to make you mine. I had to wait until I was in my late twenties. I have the utmost confidence that Frankie knows what he needs to do."

Kiera bit her lip then smiled. "I guess you're right. If Frankie was willing to give up his precious iPad, a device that allows him to talk to the world, for a girl he's just met, there has to be more there than just a schoolboy crush."

"Exactly."

"I can't wait to see this play out," Kiera commented.

"Me either. And hopefully we'll have a front row seat for the next ten years."

"Or more," Kiera added. "You did tell him that

she might want to go to college or do something else when she's eighteen."

"So I did." Cooper leaned over Frankie and pulled Kiera to him with a hand behind her neck. He kissed her quickly then sat back.

"What are we going to tell his dad?" Kiera asked.

Cooper smirked. "Nothing. Let's let him figure it out on his own."

"Figure what out?"

"That his seven-year-old son just met the girl he wants to marry."

Kiera smiled and shook her head. "He wouldn't believe us anyway."

"True. Very true."

Hours later, after the plane had landed, and after Frankie's dad had greeted them and given his son the camera he'd purchased on behalf of Annie, and when the father and son were on their way home, Frankie's dad signed, "So you had a good trip?"

Frankie responded, "Yeah, Dad. It was life changing." Then he held the plastic case with the army man doll in it closer to his chest and smiled. Huge.

———

Annie doesn't have a story out...yet, but as I said in

the author note at the beginning, I *am* planning on writing it.

If this was your first introduction to Annie, you can read her story in *Rescuing Emily* which is book 2 in the Delta Force Heroes series. She's in pretty much every book after that one too (And she graces the cover of *Marrying Emily*, so make sure to check that one out too!)

Also by Susan Stoker

Delta Force Heroes Series

Rescuing Rayne

Assisting Aimee - Loosely related to DF

Rescuing Emily

Rescuing Harley

Marrying Emily

Rescuing Kassie

Rescuing Bryn

Rescuing Casey

Rescuing Sadie (April 2018)

Rescuing Wendy (May 2018)

Rescuing Mary (Oct 2018)

Badge of Honor: Texas Heroes Series

Justice for Mackenzie

Justice for Mickie

Justice for Corrie

Justice for Laine (novella)

Shelter for Elizabeth

Justice for Boone

Shelter for Adeline

Shelter for Sophie

Justice for Erin

Justice for Milena (Mar 2018)

Shelter for Blythe (June 2018)
Justice for Hope (Sept 2018)
Shelter for Quinn (TBA)
Shelter for Koren (TBA)
Shelter for Penelope (TBA)

Ace Security Series

Claiming Grace
Claiming Alexis
Claiming Bailey
Claiming Felicity (Feb 2018)

Mountain Mercenaries Series

Defending Allye (Aug 2018)
Defending Chloe (Dec 2018)
more to come!

SEAL of Protection Series

Protecting Caroline
Protecting Alabama
Protecting Fiona
Marrying Caroline (novella)
Protecting Summer
Protecting Cheyenne
Protecting Jessyka
Protecting Julie (novella)
Protecting Melody

Protecting the Future
Protecting Alabama's Kids (novella)
Protecting Kiera (novella)
Protecting Dakota

Stand Alone
The Guardian Mist
Nature's Rift
A Princess for Cale
A Moment in Time- A Collection of Short Stories

Special Operations Fan Fiction
http://www.stokeraces.com/kindle-worlds.html

Beyond Reality Series
Outback Hearts
Flaming Hearts
Frozen Hearts

Writing as Annie George:
Stepbrother Virgin (erotic novella)

ABOUT THE AUTHOR

New York Times, USA Today, and *Wall Street Journal* Bestselling Author Susan Stoker has a heart as big as the state of Texas where she lives, but this all American girl has also spent the last fourteen years living in Missouri, California, Colorado, and Indiana. She's married to a retired Army man who now gets to follow *her* around the country.

She debuted her first series in 2014 and quickly followed that up with the SEAL of Protection Series, which solidified her love of writing and creating stories readers can get lost in.

If you enjoyed this book, or any book, please consider leaving a review. It's appreciated by authors more than you'll know.

www.stokeraces.com
susan@stokeraces.com

facebook.com/authorsusanstoker

twitter.com/Susan_Stoker

instagram.com/authorsusanstoker

goodreads.com/SusanStoker

bookbub.com/authors/susan-stoker

amazon.com/author/susanstoker

Manufactured by Amazon.ca
Bolton, ON

37018672R00076